I0554251

DARK MATH CHRONICLES

RUNTIME ZERO

Streaming the New Infinity

Mick Brady

ISBN-10: 0-996-88620-6

ISBN-13: 978-0-996-88620-8

Praise for
Runtime Zero:

"Sandpaper prose to scrape the cheap paint off your mind."
—Alan Kaufman, novelist, poet, and editor of
The Outlaw Bible of American Literature

"Spontaneous bebop prosody for the 21st Century."
—Bruce Daniels, editor, *Albuquerque Journal*

*"Runtime Zero propels the reader into an imaginative world
with a personal story that will long be remembered."*
—James D. McFarlin, author, *Aftershock: A Novel*

*"If James Joyce dropped acid
and wrote a sci-fi novel, this would be it."*
—Robert Brady, author, *The Big Elsewhere*

To Liz, my real-life Juliette,
who finally taught me how to fly

CONTENTS

I saw the angel in the marble
and I carved until I set him free.
—Michelangelo Buonarotti

1

SUBVERSA

Even before he stepped from the swirling pillar of mist in Sandbox 12, Chrome could feel himself shrinking in the face of a great emptiness, as if his identity had been checked at the door like a wet raincoat. By rezzing into a digital body, he had voluntarily surrendered most of the reference points that were central to his sense of self in the atomic world. Now the old soul, the booster rocket, the Will Powers imprint, was falling back to Earth, and with it many of the things he once measured himself by, things that had given him substance and stature in the other life. The loss of this mental skeleton left him floundering like a jellyfish in a Texas roadhouse. "Helluva way to start the day for a master of the universe," he said to no one.

Sandbox 12 was a great, flat, smooth expanse of blinding-white sand stretching as far as the eye could see, an immense chamber of silence presided over by an almost tangible blue void with nary a cloud in sight. A great copper disk hovered low on the horizon, roiled by a layer of visually convincing heat waves. In direct contrast to his life as a breather, he now felt his very soul being sucked out into the desert air, leaving him empty, aching, and struggling to understand *why,* after all those years of preparation, he had been thrust into such a desolate point of entry. This wasn't the paradise he had been looking for.

Recalling one of the bullet points from his orientation in the training chamber, he swiped his hand in the air and a luminous display appeared, clear as crystal and studded with an array of options. One click brought up an instant overview of the local grid, providing the names, locations, and profiles of any other avatars in the area, whether they were sky dwellers, diggers, or flat-out surface monkeys. Damned if the map wasn't just as barren as the landscape itself. "Hell, I might as well be adrift in outer space," he thought, as a dying star slammed into the horizon with a dull thud.

Zooming out on the map, he noticed a small yellow dot crawling across the grid from the far corner of the northeast quadrant, and when he glanced up over the screen, he spotted a plume of dust headed his way. Double clicking on the dot got him a close-up of the vehicle, a classic '64 Alfa Romeo GTV, dusty silver, along with a brief profile of its driver, a dazzling diva wrapped tightly in the lacy doublet of an Elizabethan courtier.

Name: *Quintessential Flux*

Genus: *Motherlord*

The rest was mind candy. He was good to go by the time she got there, and when she did, the very arc and vapor of his new life blew right through him.

***

The yellow dot soon became a silver juggernaut, sliding sideways toward him in a cloud of dust, finally coming to rest within inches of his new feet. Before he could even look inside, the driver reached over and opened the door.

"Welcome to SubVersa, Chrome. Hop in."

"Thanks for the lift, umm…" he said, banging his head as he climbed in, his sleek metal hair ringing like a silver bell. "Sorry; can't seem to keep track of my body in here."

"Don't worry; you'll get used to it in no time. I've been looking forward to meeting you." He was soon awash in her smiling eyes, a vast azure sea for a soul to swim in, and beginning to feel a hunger for things he didn't even know existed.

"Wow…thanks…a few more minutes and you would have had to pick me up with a shovel."

She began to explain why his internal landscape had been erased, pointing out that if he had entered this world with his human identity intact, he would have disintegrated like a chunk of space debris hitting the earth's atmosphere. Fortunately, most of the impurities of his previous life had been removed before he even reached the training chamber.

"Yeah, I get it; a clean reboot. Theoretically, then, I should run a lot smoother in here," he said, beaming at her. When she didn't respond, he said, "Say, what's your username again?"

"Call me Quin."

"Thanks, Quin." He glanced around at the leather and wood interior. "Very impressive," he thought to himself. "Just like the one my maker wrapped around a streetlight one night back on planet Earth."

"Yes, I'm familiar with the story of your maker,"

she said, startling him. "This is yours, by the way; I threw it together this morning. Something familiar, something to soften the landing."

"You *made* this? For *me?* I'm speechless. How can I thank you?"

"My pleasure, really. But don't worry, Chrome; there'll be plenty of opportunities to thank me. Ready to explore?"

"Explore? Seems like I've seen it all just by standing on my tiptoes."

"In here, nothing is as it seems. It's a shimmering world of reimaginings, a land of liquid energy. Hang on." He was suddenly thrust back against the red leather seat as the Alfa rocketed forward, lifting off the desert floor and banking sharply toward the falling sun. They were closing in on twilight.

As it was in the original world, the sun grew brighter as they raced it to the horizon. Far below, vivid ribbons of color began to appear on the desert floor, filigree rippling in the heat, shifting, changing as they soared over them. The ribbons became a pattern which grew, twisted, and churned until it blossomed into its full-blown interlocking glory: a giant, sprawling, multihued mandala, as big as a small city. As they descended in a soft downward spiral, it soon became clear that this was a *real* sand painting, the very metaphor for impermanence, on a scale unimaginable.

To top it off, sitting smack dab in the middle of it all, like a cherry on a cake, was a full-on midcentury American carnival, complete with carousels, roller coasters, calliopes, and cotton candy, and teeming with vintage avatars. The Alfa touched down like a feather just outside the entrance to the midway, and it was there, between the broad bands of red and gold sand, in the whirling dust and shadow of the Ferris wheel, to the tinny sound of an organ grinder, that Chrome got his first taste of life in this new world. He was instantly and utterly intoxicated.

2

THE MAKER

Will arrived in Manhattan during the age of sorcery known as the Sixties, flush from all the crush and buzz surrounding his incendiary *Hells Angel* painting, hailed by critics as "an homage to protean sexual power and visceral freedom," and so on. Once that first intoxicating whiff of fame had taken hold, visions of a celestial city began to dance in his head like a spaceship all aglitter, with God and William Blake at the helm, beaming rays of hope into the damp darkness of his dreams.

One summer morn, after a night of sweat and disappointment, he arose from his lover's bed and slipped behind the wheel of a dusty blue VW bus crammed with oozing tubes of acrylic paint, coffee cans full of paint-frosted brushes, rolls of raw canvas, gallons of gesso; books, more books, and the finest jazz collection a starving artist could buy. He was headed south, down the New York State Thruway, to Gotham, to the Emerald City, to Babylon...the first level of the inferno.

***

That first, bewitching summer, Will found himself in a swirling whirl of artists, musicians, poets, hippies, and street wizards, all randomly tossed into the East Village stew with the last big wave of immigrants—ethnic Ukrainians, mostly, the only ones who weren't perpetually stoned, a sturdy tribe who stoically tolerated the growing circus in their midst, biding their time until it was their turn to step out into the American Dream.

After a few months of floating around town, staying with friends, scrambling for cash, and hunting for a space, he stumbled onto an empty storefront on 10th Street off Tompkins Square, right around the corner from the Peace Eye Bookstore, where Ed Sanders and Allen Ginsberg were writing the script for the coming revolution. He built a sleeping loft in the back room behind the kitchen and began working in the wide-open space of the storefront. The ancient brick walls were soon checkered with canvases, the well-worn floors spattered with paint. A beat-up old coffeepot bubbled in the background, brewing an endless batch of fuel for his fertile mind.

A river of morning light cascaded in from the street, bouncing off the smooth wooden floors, filling in the spaces with warmth and energy. It seemed to set the paintings ablaze, drawing a moveable sea of faces to the big window, faces that followed his every move as he worked on the giant canvases. This small, rapt audience turned the studio into a kind of street theater, his fevered painting into a kind of performance art. The music pounding through his homegrown speakers provided each new painting with its own soundtrack and a backbeat for his flying feet. Having traded drumsticks for paintbrushes, the former drummer for The Bravados was now painting with the colors of rhythm and blues, 'cause, hey, man, you paint pretty for the people, you just might get you some *sat-is-fac-tion.*

***

Some mornings, Mona Lisa came padding out of the back room in Will's old Syracuse sweatshirt, half awake, cradling a cup of coffee, strolling right through the cluttered studio and out onto the sidewalk to talk to one of their new friends, one of the regulars, one of those she knew by name. Will didn't mind; when he was buried in a painting he was gone, real gone, and she truly knew he'd rather *make* art than talk about it. And so there she was, the girl he'd once traded for the big city, keeping up his end of the conversation while he provided color commentary. Love was full of surprises.

There were always two or three paintings going at once, the maxim being to keep one alive while the others dried. The look was tough; the tone, high contrast; the feel, blunt, romantic, and unambiguous; the style, urban pop. He painted machines in motion—cars, trucks, bicycles, motorcycles—all turning, twisting, as if trying to break free of the canvas and careen into another world.

"Wonder where the hell they're goin'," Royko, a neighbor and fellow artist, once said. "Wherever it is, man, it sure looks like they're dying to get there."

Will thought for a minute. "They're headed straight for your mind's eye at the speed of light, Royko, which tends to bend around a curve, lending the illusion of danger; but it's the poor souls in Grant Wood's painting who are really dying to get there," he said. A print of *Death on Ridge Road*, one of

Will's favorite works, was hanging in the back room.

"Your head's on fire, man, you know that? Your… fucking…head…is on *fire*." Royko looked at him for a minute, then walked away, grinning.

Will had been drawing his getaway dreams since the day his bike was stolen from behind the Delaware Theater while he and his brother were rooting for the good guys at a Saturday matinee. As he stood there in the alley that day, thunderstruck at the magnitude of his loss, he realized that his last, best hope of outrunning his demons was gone. In this new, cold reality, there would never be another chance to fly.

This, just weeks after his father ran off with the perfume lady at Whitney's department store, where he was the window display man. Will was still reeling from those final, tearful moments with his dad before he pulled out of the VFW Post parking lot in their new '49 Merc headed for Reno while Will stood there, collapsing inwardly like a slo-mo demolition, tumbling all the way down into his shoes. He was left staring into a billowing cloud of dust as his father missed the driveway by a couple of feet and careened, bumping and lurching, out of his life forever. The cloud was all that remained.

His family soon migrated to the slums and, before long, they pawned everything they owned, including his beloved hunting knife with the twelve-point buck etched right into the blade, all majestic under the waterfall. It was a last, desperate attempt to avoid the crushing shame of welfare, but after a few long, hungry weeks, there they were, hats in hand, shuffling together down the long gray hallways of the social services center. By then, the only thing he had left was the untested power of his imagination.

Drawing a fleet of low-slung chariots—sleek, sinewy, fire-breathing monsters that pounded their tires in the dust—became a handy way to avoid locking himself in the bathroom at night with the one thing his dad had left behind in his blind flight to freedom—a rusty old Gillette blue blade. Fighting pain with pain, he tried to bleed out the demons that were hissing in his ear, insisting he was the one who drove his father out the door. On one of those nights, the mix of blood and water circling the drain triggered a memory of his father stumbling into the kitchen in the middle of the night, living-dead drunk, soaking wet, and covered with blood after falling facedown into the wading pool on his way home from the Post. As Will watched this last, bittersweet memory run down the drain, he decided it was better to get lost in layers of hand-rubbed cherry lacquer on a pretty little roadster or tease apart the shadows on a full moon hubcap, than to carve another notch in his arm. Life was tough, but dreams were free, and drawing a fleet of dream machines was an easy way to tweak a poorly designed universe.

He didn't know it then, but those drawings were the prototypes of the mind rockets that would one day set him free. Those graphite roadsters with fat black tires and silver wheels had the power to erase all memory of his stripped-down gunmetal bike, setting his dreams in motion. They were the imaginary chariots of his future, like the Alfa coupe he would wrap around a pole in the drunken-hearted sadness and madness of his Black Irish youth, or the cherry-red Triumph that would carry him, floating, into Woodstock on a cloud of ganja. They were the early blueprints of his midnight rides in the Mothership, and finally, they were a foreshadowing of the phantom motorcycle that would one day carry his digital angel into the heart of Babylon. He was building a fleet of spiritual machines, longing for lift-off.

Some months later, after one decidedly joyous session in the studio—a time when the whole world seemed to disappear—he stood back, surveyed all that he had done, and saw that it was good. There was light, and there was darkness. There was motion, and there was stillness. There was strength and weakness, joy and sadness. But above all, there was a window to another world—a land of light and shadow that any one of these chariots could reach at a moment's notice.

Why this was so, he didn't know. But he hadn't yet seen the celestial city hovering in the clouds above him as he lay suspended, dream-floating on the surface of a blue mountain lake. He hadn't yet heard the poem at the center of the universe, or learned that the stars were fueled by the same energy that ran through his mind. Then, and only then, would it become clear that all God's children were angels trapped within a ring of fire, and one by one, Will would take them home.

3

QUANTUM ART

"It's like dancing with angels. Just let go, and it'll flow," Juliette said, one foot bouncing off her knee as she lay stretched out on the floor of the art cube.

Chrome, sitting with his back against the chopper, glanced over with a smile, then buried himself once more in the tedious task of scanning image codes on the airscreen. "If only it were that simple," he thought. The Quantum Art exhibit was just weeks away, and he was losing focus. His mind was adrift in the ebb and flow of long ago, whispers of other worlds streaming through his head in an endless loop—tantalizing bits of data, agonizingly familiar, virtually indecipherable. He had to let go, kick himself back into gear, and get on with his work. This would be his last show in SubVersa, and there was no time for daydreaming.

The art cube itself was as big as a couple of cargo containers, every wall covered with a riotous carnival of nude drawings, splattered paint and bullet-riddled sheet metal, an iconic banana logo floating in the center like an erotic piñata. There were no shadows in here; each surface was its own source of light, evoking a dizzying sense of weightlessness, erasing all sense of direction. Chrome and his muse were immersed in a work of art.

They had been cooped up in here for days, searching for a way to spark the creative fire that might burn down the wall between SubVersa and the original world and, in the process, shed some light on the forces that had shaped them. They were avatars, an artist and his muse, but more than that, they were works of art themselves, and they were about to embark on a mission that had begun long ago in a place called Manhattan, a legendary citadel that had forged their own maker. Though they didn't know it yet, the first inklings of that mission were beginning to trickle in on the daydream channel.

Juliette Q45 had arrived a few weeks earlier; a noob, a newborn avatar, a code warrior princess sprung from the mind of her maker like Athena leaping from the head of Zeus, fully intact and ready for action. In addition to possessing all the magical powers of a muse, she could take out a rogue avi with a samurai sword if she had to, but there were better ways to disarm it—a deadly embrace, for instance; a different kind of action and a much quicker, much sweeter way to go.

Chrome, on the other hand, was a stone worn smooth from years of slipstreaming the grid; he was a far cry from the guy who first stepped out of the mist in Sandbox 12 stamped with the prefab look shared by all avatars in those days, a new recruit in an army of mannequins. As tech aesthetics improved, he was incrementally upgraded, eventually morphing into a new breed of street surfer. Maori tattoos *("Polynesian pin-striping")* under a satin cowboy shirt adorned with hand-painted pinup girls *("my satin dolls")*, a pair of black string jeans over boots of hand-tooled leather and, his crowning glory, a gleaming halo of metal hair that captured all the colors of the rainbow, including those only his dog Proto could see.

They lived in a world that was about as close as one could get to the afterlife while still breathing. It was the most expansive, the most malleable, and the most reliable of them all; a creative fantasyland where the liquid self could be endlessly reinvented, where an artist could finally break free of those pesky laws of physics. It was a boot camp for the soul, a prep school for paradise. It was the mind made manifest, a land beyond language, the virtual world of SubVersa.

It was here that Chrome had achieved his maker's dream of becoming a master artist. And it was here that he led his ragtag band of gearheads on midnight runs through the Underzone looking for trouble. Wherever they found it, they refiggered it, rejiggered it, and soundly put the jam on it with random acts of creative genius. They were the Code Warriors, champions of an open-source society fueled by creative energy. They were militant realists, pragmatic poets, creative evolutionaries who had passed through the fires of hell and emerged as strong and flexible as tempered steel. They were in sync with the Master Code, and they were ready to roll, leaning hard to the wild side of the solid white line that ran through the universe. The motto emblazoned on their backs was a nod to their origins and to their calling: *In Numero Vero* (Truth In Numbers).

They were arch enemies of the head-spiked Alien Nomads, a roving band of free radicals who lived life in reverse and would suck the light right out of you in a matter of seconds, if you let 'em. Griefers. Fades. Mindwolves. Chrome and his crew were among the very few who could scan their mathnicity in the dark and shut them down with a searing burst of bebop mind jamming. In a virtual world, where there are no limits to the power of the imagination, a well-timed art bomb was like a flower in the barrel of a gun, tamping down the darkness with a shaft of light.

One moonless autumn night, Chrome and his gang of creative pirates turned a potentially deadly suckfest into an all-night rave, simply by rezzing a holographic slampunk concert right in the middle of Chernobyl Street. Everyone got out alive, and the Warriors left with one more notch on their belts and a three-mile smile from all the free beers and high fives down at the Savoy Truffle.

***

Chrome stood up, walked to the center of the cube, rezzed a beat-up old Magnavox hi-fi set, and then turned slowly toward his languishing muse, as a dusty vinyl record dropped onto the turntable. He offered his hand, she accepted gracefully, and they were soon swimming in the inky depths of a song by Sonny Boy Williamson, still aching to bring it on home to his honey-babe in the dark of some south-side Chicago bar, circa 1963. "Welcome to eternity," Chrome whispered in her ear.

"Mmm…*so* good to be home," she said, burrowing in even deeper. Then, as the song began to fade, she raised her head, violet eyes shining. "Speaking of eternity, Chrome, can I ask you something?"

"Sure, babe; fire away."

"When I'm with you, everything is as clear as a bell, but when I'm alone, it feels as if I don't exist. I seem to be sitting on the edge of my future, but there's no past to fall back on. Can you tell me where all this begins?"

Chrome thought long and hard before answering. "For us, there *is* no past until we create it. It begins and ends within the mind of our creator, but we have to gain access to that data for ourselves and make it our own. Fortunately, every bit and pixel of human history is embedded in a universal database called the space-time continuum, including the story of our origins, which is pretty much the story of our maker," he said, looking at her intently.

"But how do we get there from here?"

"That's what I've been trying to figure out. I have a few clues, but in the meantime, the best I can do is share the bits and pieces handed down to me over the years, if that would help. One thing I do know, though, is that paradise came at a very high price, and that Will Powers had to pass through the inferno to get us here."

"So, what you're saying is we have to go out and track down our own past?" she said, ignoring his offer. She was not the type to accept hand-me-downs.

"Pretty much. But it's not as easy as you might think, Jules; it begins in another world, another century."

"Well, what are we waiting for then?" she said, crossing her arms to cover her excitement.

Chrome mounted the Harley, kick-starting the beast into a snarling roar. "Hop on, sweet thing; let's run this fantasy down."

***

The chopper shot through the phantom wall like a bullet through a box of shadows. Juliette hung on tightly as they reached the edge of the platform and lifted off into the sky, cruising high above a bank of clouds in one of the more remote parts of the metasphere, the sun all pink and lazy and sinking like a stone—which it does four times a day in SubVersa, unless someone puts it to bed early for personal reasons, as lovers often do.

Far below, in the pulsating streets of Blue City, nubile young pixies, preening steampunk poets, and scruffy cyberartists were hard at play, each on one side of a double life, straddling two worlds, living on the final frontier at the edge of human identity. Their mortals were scattered across the outer world, empowering the souls that made up this freewheeling creative beehive. "*Needle in the Groove*," Chrome suddenly called out, his voice code triggering the automatic landing system as they approached the gallery runway.

There were two landing pads on the roof, one already occupied by a rocket plane, well worn from the days of the Gorean Wars. The other was wide open, its landing lights blinking in the dwindling twilight. The chopper dropped, lurching slightly, onto the rubberized metal surface. As he killed the engine, the lattice grid they rested on began to descend into the gallery—a cavernous rocket hangar recycled from a now-defunct Star Wars sim.

High above the hangar door, a neon logo flickered into the deepening night: 'Art From Inner Space,' Chrome Underwood's personal gallery, the center of gravity for his wide-ranging creative activities. As the platform settled silently onto the floor of the vast enclosure, they stepped onto a surface beribboned with the lucent pattern of a giant circuit board. Light was the source of all life in here; Chrome was born to reflect it.

Juliette circled the floor of the old hangar, feasting on each painting in turn. A lightsphere drone with full AI hovered nearby, ready to answer any questions, but there was no need; she was a walking database of human art history, ranging from the first cave paintings at Altamira to the latest dreambabies of the hypermodernists—including the deep context that drove it home. She also knew exactly where Chrome belonged in the pantheon. The artist himself, meanwhile, stood nearby, deeply moved by the grace in every ripple of her skintight leathers. At long last, she turned and spoke.

"All the beauty and brutality of humanity wrapped up in such a pretty bow. Is this your gift to the mother planet?"

"Better to give than to receive," he said, smiling warmly. She smiled back.

"Critics describe it as 'visual punk,' and 'intellectual anarchy,'" she said as she stood before his massive three-dimensional painting, *Rock/Star/ Gravity*. "But I think they're missing the point. Certainly your work is as dangerous as anything in the database, but it also hints at something bigger, something brighter—a way out of the deep, dark forest of human history, perhaps? How could they have missed the shimmering hope in these pictures?"

"Humanity sees through a glass darkly, it's true," he replied. "But even here in SubVersa, we're still works in progress, you know; many things remain invisible, just out of reach. You, on the other hand, happen to be an advanced muse. Not much is hidden from you."

"Thank you, Sir Chrome. But let's not forget that it was you who taught me how to see around corners," she said. He couldn't help but smile.

"The credit actually belongs to our maker, Will Powers, who came by his wisdom the hard way, scorched by the refining fire."

"And, if I'm not mistaken, you get to harvest the fruit of his suffering?"

"Only at his behest, darlin', and only in this world… so far, at least. In the other world, this is all part of a much larger artwork, and so are we."

"Wait…What do you mean, exactly?"

"Well, in this slice of reality, we're the stars in his movie, living facets of his imagination; as such, we're about as close as a human artist can get to *pure thought* as an art medium. Here in SubVersa, we're his living ideas, and I'm his primary surrogate, the artist he once dreamed of becoming, a virtual art star. Where it all ends, nobody knows."

"Hmm…a legend in his own mind. All well and good for you, perhaps, but what does that make me? His master's handmaiden?"

"No, no, *no*, dear Juliette. You are the embodiment of the classical ideal of beauty, the sine qua non in this equation; you are my muse, my vitamin Q, the spark that lights my fire."

With a disarming look of heart-fluttering innocence, she stood on her tiptoes, wrapped her arms around his shoulders, and planted a big, wet kiss on his neck. Then, nibbling at his earlobe, she whispered, "You mean like this, Chromeo?"

"Mmhmm…yeah…that too." For one brief, incandescent moment, they coalesced into a single, throbbing field of energy, setting hearts and dishes all a-clatter on the terraform below.

***

Nestled behind the gallery was a long, narrow room which could only be accessed through a phantom painting hanging on the back wall, a room where space jockeys once lingered between interstellar flights and romantic dalliances. Now it was Chrome's inner sanctum. At the far end of the dimly lit chamber, light pods hovered over the imposing figure of a Hells Angel on his chopper, exploding across the canvas as though he was storming the pearly gates on a bolt of lightning.

"Wow. Looks like you in a previous life. Is it?" Juliette was staring wide-eyed at the painting.

"I might be the glimmer in his eyes…I think we come from the same family tree."

"How's that?" she asked cautiously.

"Will Powers, the mind on the other side, the one who created us, was swept into a big city by this painting many years ago, which led to his own wild journey to the edge of existence and beyond, to a new kind of creative redemption. I think that's really him in the painting, born and raised in hell and running flat out for the gates of heaven. He didn't quite make it, but man, what a ride. He could've given Icarus a run for his money."

Juliette, wild child of imagination that she was, had already left the building on the back of that dream machine while Chrome rambled on unawares. She found herself cruising through mindspace with the Angel, inexorably drawn toward the sound of an old delta blues tune—a beacon set in place by the creator himself, that she might bear witness to the days and nights he had spent marooned on an island called Manhattan, in the Year of Our Lord, One Thousand Nine Hundred and Sixty-Eight.

4

THE MOTHERSHIP

Will was slouched behind the wheel of his grimy yellow cab, its windshield hazy from the splattered mist of a midmorning shower. He'd spent the last hour or so riding a wave of green lights up and down the island in a series of twenty- or thirty-block ellipses, angling for fares, finally catching red at 52nd, where he sat tapping his hands to the primal call of the mighty Son House on WBAI, absentmindedly scanning the streets for the next warm body.

Tell me who's that writin', John the Revelator
Tell me who's that a-writin', John the Revelator
Wrote the book of the seven seals

This used to be a fine time to think—a mindless cruise to nowhere on a Saturday morning, a much-needed break from doing battle with a blank canvas, a chance for the mind to run off leash. But in this new version of reality, art in all its rainbow glory was no more than a distant memory. He hadn't finished a painting in months, hadn't had a show in over a year. He was now a living creative block, solid as a stone Buddha, and he was in grave danger. He knew the kryptonite hovering just outside his head could bring him down at any moment, and he knew he couldn't stop it any more than he could lift a fog with his bare hands. But he also knew that if he could *just keep moving*, one tragic moment at a time, he could outrun the messenger of death. Of this he was certain, for it had been revealed to him in a dream by the desolation angel himself, St. Jacques de Kerouac, patron saint of boho travelers.

Will's constant motion was fueled by an endless supply of ganja from the mystic gardens of Tibet—exquisite spliffs that magically appeared from a thicket of curls the color of chocolate rolling paper, a sacred space forever safe from the groping fingers of the law. Thus did he stay high all day, every day, for months and months on end—a particular point of pride among the tribes of East Freakistan.

Then one fateful summer eve, on their way home from Provincetown, he and Ave Maria dropped some Sunshine on the hallowed lawns of Harvard Yard (a touchstone in the culture of consciousness still under the luminous spell of Dr. Timothy Leary, who was by then a major constellation in the midnight sky), and time—time itself—began to melt like Dalí's clock, morphing into something infinitely more erotic and exotic than the endless shuffling from one moment to another in the world they'd left behind. They were starborn, traveling light-years together beneath the trees, soaring from one breath to another, pressed hard against the soft green surface of the earth, butterflies dreaming.

***

But then, alas, he had to return to the city, where there was little room for dreams. It was, in fact, booked solid with nightmares. Hallucinations now slipped in and out of his head like wolves in a snow-covered forest, popping up out of nowhere, choking him with fear, then slinking away as quickly as they had appeared. "Many are cold, but few are frozen," Freddie the Flute once said; "and when you can't see the forest for the wolves, that's when it all goes black." As Will knew all too well, many of his fellow tribesmen were already deep in the forest, and some would never make it out alive. He was on high alert.

The greater danger, of course, was reality itself. You never knew when one of those visions might come bubbling up out of nowhere, uncoiling into life like that little junkie who jumped into his cab on 23rd Street before he even had a chance to scope him out. Eyes like Ping-Pong balls, sweating like a snake handler, gun aimed right at the back of Will's head.

In those days, there was nothing between the cabby and his passenger; they were alone together on a floating island, the fare no more than a face in the mirror, a cipher in the backseat. All this, while slipstreaming through traffic like a dolphin in a shiver of sharks. Some drivers took protective measures like checking out each fare before popping the door, or slipping a blunt object under the front seat before leaving the garage; others, it was said, were packing heat. Will rode bravely into battle with nothing but his trusty radio by his side, music being his first line of defense in any crisis.

"Where ya headed, my friend?" Will asked, calm, cool, collected.

"If you make one false move, motherfucker, I'll

splatter your brains all over the roof of your cab. Take me uptown."

"Yes, sir, you got it, my friend."

What he got was a long ride up and down the island, a brief eternity in a grimy yellow cab, which soon became a tear-stained confessional, with Will his drug-stained confessor. Will had a way with words when he was stoned to the bone and amped on adrenaline, and by the time that desperado finally decided to jump ship and blend into the crowd at Grand Central, he had a fair amount of cash and a contact high, plenty to get him to his next fix. They parted like old friends.

But the number and frequency of these eruptions were climbing, and his head was getting mighty crowded. Like the gang of subway bikers that jumped him when he and Mona Lisa were walking past the tilted steel cube at Cooper Union. Will, a seasoned veteran of the streets, quickly sized them up as posers, Hells Angels wannabes, street punks who couldn't afford to buy their own choppers and lived out their toxic fantasies on the subway trains of New York.

A lean, glassy-eyed stripling stepped up and

grabbed him by his T-shirt and demanded his denim jacket. As Will began to resist, an otherwise ordinary fellow stepped out of the crowd and said, right up next to his head in a deep whisper, "Don't you know who these guys are? They're the Savage Dolls. They set a guy on fire over on 4th Street just to watch him burn. Made page three in the *Times*. Not worth a lousy jacket, man." Then he backed away.

"You know something, man? You make a damn good point," Will said, looking at him over the alien's shoulder. After handing over his jacket, he and Mona Lisa slipped into the crowd on St. Mark's Place, now a mecca for the au courant, where the Exploding Plastic Inevitable was headlining at the Electric Circus. Its midway made the perfect getaway scene.

Their mood was lightened by a delirious romp in front of the Cosmic Blues record shop, where the thundering swamp music of Creedence Clearwater had ignited a spontaneous tribal dance that spilled out onto the street, pulling in all who passed by. From a poster in the store window, a smiling Dylan was tipping his hat to the dancing crowd, a gesture not lost on Will. "All is right with the world," he thought. "The sorcerer is smiling."

And yet there seemed to be no limit to the ill will of his fellow man, whose true nature, unbeknownst to Will, was held hostage to the seven deadly settings of an ancient virus. Within days, he would be mugged at midnight in Tompkins Square Park by a spoon monkey holding a broken bottle to his throat. Or the dog day in July when a band of Arabs swarmed his cab on Pier 26 after an international dispute over the fare, forcing him to throttle down with one of them still on the hood. Will dropped him off at the other end with a delicate swerve and a light tap on the brakes; no harm done, no extra charge. But it was further proof of the growing darkness, as if he were caught up in a war no one else seemed to notice. Day after day, he circled the island in the Mothership, running recon on the front lines of the revolution, with no particular place to go.

These reveries were suddenly interrupted by a dazzling array of sunlight on the wet pavement outside his cab. Before the light changed, he flipped his last Lucky Strike out the window and watched as it landed on the rainbow surface of an oil slick, creating an instant color field painting, like a miniature Morris Louis. "Maybe I should switch to oils," he said to himself as he gunned the yellow beast back into the river of traffic. Then, "Nah, the fumes'll kill ya."

5

BREATHERS

Juliette clung tightly to the Angel as the bike plunged through the surface of the mindzone with a jagged clap of thunder, its fat rear tire greeting mother earth with a blossom of blue smoke, the front end feathering down like a rocket plane on a gripstone runway. They were rolling fast under a broad sweep of trees in a canyon of glass and steel, headed straight for a skyscraper that stood astride the road like a mighty colossus.

"In a solid world, you must find an opening in a surface before attempting to pass through it. High-speed contact can be fatal for a human," Chrome once said. Her train of thought was instantly throttled by what sounded like a shotgun blast, as the Angel began a series of rapid downshifts. Leaning hard into the first curve, they began snaking among the massive columns supporting the building and, within seconds, exploded from the other side, headed south. Juliette was thrilled right down to her wireframe boots.

"This is not just a solid world; this is a *hard* world," she thought. An immovable, impenetrable world, one fundamentally different from the land of light she hailed from. It seemed to be running a graphically seamless program of impeccable beauty, fueled by a heavier form of energy—a lumbering power of fire and smoke, noise, and heat, giving back precious little light. She glanced up at the slender slice of sky above their heads. "By any reckoning, a meager portion for a multitude," she thought.

She could feel the new energy in the sudden snarl of the machine she rode on; it was there in the lingering smell of passion and decay in the streets, its throbbing noise and frantic motion hammering at her very soul. It was a living, breathing, menacing kind of force, yet, somehow, in spite of it all, she felt strangely at home and couldn't wait to get back to tell Chrome. But not until she had witnessed its full power.

There was something else bubbling up inside her, something unknown in SubVersa: she felt the blood rush that comes with a sense of impending body death, a thrill in the face of danger. She was now very close to being mortal; her neural network was running a virtual stream similar to the blood and adrenaline cocktail at the center of human existence. She was cranked, full throttle, yet fully aware that this was only a whiff of what it must be like to actually live in this world. "These poor souls are trapped down here," she said into the wind as the chopper thundered down Park Avenue. "They lack the power of reimagining, the magic of creative programming. The only way out for them is death...or madness."

As far as she knew, no one in SubVersa had ever experienced anything like it, except maybe Quin, who seemed to have been everywhere and perhaps always had been. But not even the digital doomers of the Wasteland or the synthetically hardened denizens of the Underzone had ever faced a world such as this, a place where, in the end, the body betrays the young at heart. The most they'd ever had to deal with was a cyberattack by the Nomads or maybe a glitch in the program.

But even in the event of a snow crash, when their bitmapped world turned to gibberish, it was only a matter of minutes before the lights were back on, and they were resurrected. In fact, unless the global grid went down, the program could always be rebooted;

the Code Warriors would see to that. And one day, perhaps even the threat of a grid failure would disappear, once the clouds were turned into servers, and their lives were fueled by the eternal light of the sun. For the moment, however, she was locked in a world of blood and concrete.

For her, it would be a hell of a ride, but for Will, it was the end of the road, the place where his dreams came to die. She knew the story; she saw much of it as she passed through the umbilical cord connecting mother earth to the new world. This city was all spikes and hard edges; it was indifferent, even hostile, to her presence. A deadly virus seemed to have been written into the very carbon of its being, and if it ever got ahold of her soul, it would chew her up and spit her out as well. A chill ran down her spine as she steeled herself against the seductive power of its darkness, as if she were resisting a brutal lover. And she already knew how brutal it could be; she was running the most advanced AI and now had access to the old world's darkest data.

In addition, her senses were not bound by time; she could *feel* the soul of the place. In her innermost mind, she saw the river of blood, genius, and malevolent charm that had flowed through here for centuries, creating a citadel so jaded that only the wrong survived. "If Will has already begun to resist this force, he's in even greater danger," she thought. "There's no safety net, no sanctuary for neural renegades. He could die down here and become just another homicide statistic." She had to find him. She had to be by his side.

6

SHE RUN COOL

Chrome stood in front of the empty canvas, shaking his head in disbelief. Somehow, his luminous muse had blasted off into the acrylic atmosphere of the motorcycle painting with a burst of flame and a wisp of smoke. The engine's roar was still ringing in his ears, and yet it made no sense. He had studied this painting in great detail since Will bequeathed him the original file, and it never occurred to him there might be something hidden within the digital fabric, another dimension between the pixels. Even in a creative fantasyland, this fell well within the realm of impossibility.

It was ingenious, to be sure. So ingenious, in fact, that he allowed himself a measure of silent admiration in spite of his annoyance. "A masterful piece of digital magic, not the work of an amateur," he thought. But then, Juliette was molto high end, running the best tech available and tweaked to per-fection, an irrepressible force of cybernature. She was capable of anything as long as it enhanced the underlying code of the universe, the pure math powering the heavenly gyroscope. But not this.

The logical explanation, of course, was that she had somehow flipped the canvas to phantom mode and used it to return to the gallery. His first impulse, then, was to leap in after her, give her a high five for pulling off such a damn good trick, maybe even have a good laugh with her. But the canvas remained solid, unyielding. "Plenty of *there* there," he thought. "Nothing phantom about it." He was further mystified when he walked out onto the gallery floor and saw the stars blinking cold through the open hangar door with nary a soul in sight. Gripped by fear, he tried in vain to reach her; first by voice, then by chat, and finally, by mindstreaming—a short-range medium at best.

When she didn't show up on the gridmap, his fear meter pegged *hard* and a great darkness fell upon him, leaving his insides churning, burning, like a sea of hot crude. Ancient memories swirled around him like a flock of ghosts. He sank down onto the old leather couch and even deeper into his gloom, tumbling back to a long-ago night on the Blue Bayou sim—Jolene's jukebox moaning, hormones groaning, the crowd moving across the dirt floor like starlings in the midnight sky. He had been alone in his soul that night, a naked heart in a new world, when Raven stepped from the crowd and stood before him, her hand outstretched and beckoning. "Come dance with me," she said.

***

He had known a part of him was missing from the day he first emerged in Sandbox 12, and for some reason, the aching of this phantom self had only gotten stronger in the days and nights that followed. He'd often steal away from the clubs and dance halls to go off on his midnight rambles, teleporting randomly to faraway corners of the metaverse, letting his instincts lead the way. He found the still, silent beauty of an abandoned pirate ship or a crumbling lighthouse on an outcropping of rock far more beguiling, comforting— and sometimes more frightening—than a crowded dance floor.

On one of those nights, he was floating through a moonlit forest when he came upon a bewitching young wraith with luminous green skin, segments of it laced together crudely with thick neon-orange surgical thread. Her long black hair was caked in blood as she stood there swaying, rocking, moving with the grasses in the cool night breeze. He was well within range of her seductive powers—a magnetic force field tugging at his very soul. But after a brief, soul-wrenching struggle, he gathered his wits about him and pulled away. "Even in paradise, death finds a way to peddle its wares," he thought.

Or that magic midwinter morning at the bottom of the Sea of Topaz, as he was prying loose a smooth, silvery pearl, big as a coconut, from its jewel-encrusted shell, when a pair of sea nymphs astride giant seahorses pulled into his circle of light. Silent as the night, their golden hair glittering in the dancing sunlight, they circled about him for a few electric seconds, smiling shyly, then shot off into the deepening blue green, leaving him wrapped in a swirling blossom of sand, lonely and aching and filled with wonder.

The pain of his loneliness grew so acute that he finally decided to take matters into his own hands. He began crafting the ideal female form; lovingly, limb by limb, curve by curve, pixel by pixel, until she stood shimmering before him—a virtual goddess, ready to embrace and enrich him, body and soul. He was hoping that her custom AI engine, so painstakingly synced with his own personality, would make her the perfect mate—a synthetic sweetheart with everything he needed to get by. He named her Neon for the soft warm glow that radiated from her backlit skin texture.

"Look, Chrome" she said one day, after booting up." I have a body! What should I do with it?"

"Well…" he began, and before he could finish, she was wrapped around him like a mink stole, her skin cool to the touch, her mouth ablaze with tongue of fire. Other parts led directly to the source of heat and within a few sizzling nanoseconds, they were wholly intermingled in the tango of love. Thus began the ill-fated, short-lived, and ultimately tragic heartsong of the artist and his übernatural creation.

His long-simmering fantasy was to blaze across the virtual heavens with her in his arms, Superman and Lois Lane, soaring from wonderland to wonderland, touching down in places where even the ground they walked on was a work of art. He wanted her to see what he saw, feel what he felt. He wanted to wander the damp and brooding streets of Kowloon, where tiny Hello Kitties fell from the trees and floated away like children's bubbles; or lurk with her in the shadows of Electric City where stealth warriors fought their deadly battles in skyscrapers made of light; or fly away to the Garden of Earthly Delights and get lost in an ecstatic trance dance beneath the Tree of Carnal Knowledge. He wanted to know her, truly know her. He wanted to get lost in her.

But just to ease her into it, they flew down to the Wasteland in his little red Porsche roadster, parking high above the desert floor in time to catch the sunset over Allegory Mountain. For him, this cosmic drive-in was a joyous mystery, a sacred ritual, but Neon found it merely "interesting," and as soon as the last fiery pixel dropped behind a snowcapped ridge, she asked if they could go shopping.

From that moment on, his hopes were repeatedly dashed by her cool and predictable responses, and so he returned to his old and lonely ways—staying out all night, getting lost in a crowd, or wandering the metaverse alone. For, once again, there was a lingering hunger in his heart; a hunger which soon burst into a raging fire, white hot by the time Raven danced into his heart that night on the Blue Bayou sim.

And when the dancing was done, they ported back to his place to sip champagne in the luminous gardens above the studio, a roll of gypsy jazz tinkling away in the background. As it happened, a feed of virtual imagery from his personal cache of art and intimacy was streaming along one of the garden walls when an image of Neon rolled by, bringing Raven up short, looking a bit undone.

"Chrome, I just had the strangest feeling..." she said, leaning forward and setting her glass down carefully on the bloodstone floor. He lay sideways on the pile of cushions, head on hand, looking puzzled. "I'm all ears, Raven," he said.

"I think that's me!" she said, her eyes fixed on the image of Neon gliding by.

"Really? Well, then, who's the beautiful creature lying beside me?"

"No, I mean, that's the face I see in my dreams, the person I look for in the mirror every morning. The real me, the way I see myself inside. Who is she?"

He then launched into the tale of how, in the depths of his loneliness and despair, he had created Neon— from the first thrilling moments he began building her to the day he realized that she was nothing more than a finely tuned and highly charged digital doll—and how that realization left him reeling, feeling emptier than ever.

"Does she still exist?" she asked cautiously.

"Yes. She models for me, appears in many of my paintings."

"I wish I were her," she said in a faraway voice, as the silken strings of Django's guitar worked their magic in the background.

Within days, he decided to scrub the data from Neon's heart drive and turn her complete and lovely body over to Raven, which was very much like handing over the keys to a new Maserati; once she had the access code, all she had to do was hop in and drive her off the showroom floor. She did exactly that, and instantly blossomed into the woman of her dreams. It seemed to be a win-win situation at first, since Chrome was relieved that Neon, his plastic fantastic lover, was finally inhabited by a soul connected to a real woman. But as tantalizing as this arrangement was, he soon sensed the danger in it; he was no longer in complete control of his lover, and therefore anything at all was now possible. She could leave him at any moment, for instance, run off with another lover and shatter his heart like a goblet on his bloodstone floor, leaving him broken and wounded and grieving for months on end. Which, of course, she did.

7

BLEEDERS

The low-slung monster blasted its way through thick-ening traffic and rolled into midtown Manhattan, not far from where Rosenquist once painted billboards high above the teeming masses in Times Square before descending in all his glory to grace the walls of the Castelli Gallery. Within minutes, the eye-pop-ping chopper pulled alongside Will's cab as he sat in line in front of the Hotel Taft, waiting to scoop up a big tipper. Juliette leaned forward, planted a kiss on the Angel's cheek, slid from the saddle, and jumped into the front seat of the cab. In the blink of an eye, she was sitting right there beside him, beaming, as the Angel thundered away in the background. Will, still on high alert, thought it might be a setup, then quickly brushed the thought aside. "Get ahold of yourself, man," he thought, "drama's drama, but *damn*, this is one sexy mama." It was as if she had reached out and touched him with her smile.

She was beautiful—that was undeniable—but

not in any way he could ever hope to put his finger on. Her skin, for instance, that translucent alabaster skin, those violet eyes, the shock of black hair deeper than space tumbling about her face. A slim silver bar nestled on her breast and a single, luminous star dangled from her ear. Struck by her unearthly beauty, he was fully prepared to accept the possibility that he was in the presence of a goddess from another planet, still wrapped in tight black leather for her interstellar flight.

"Hi, Will. I can't believe this…that this is really *you*!" she said.

"Yeah, well, that's cool, 'cause I'm not even sure it's me half the time…But, hey…you knew my name…Who *are* you?"

"Don't have time to explain right now, but we'll get to know each other real soon, I promise. Let's just say I'm working on a very important project."

"Student? Cooper Union? NYU?"

Before she had a chance to answer, the cabby ahead of him pulled away, and as Will eased his cab up to the hotel entrance, the doorman peered into the front seat with a puzzled look on his face. "It's OK, man; we're cool," Will said, assuring him that he was there to pick up a fare regardless of the goddess riding shotgun. At that very moment, the hotel door flew open and out strode a tall Texan in a dark pinstriped suit and a white cowboy hat, a ragged leather briefcase at his side.

"Howdy, Mister!" the big Texan shouted as he reached the curb, well into his monologue before he even climbed into the backseat. "Must be a salesman," Will thought, sitting quietly, waiting for the punch line before asking where he wanted to go, smiling all the while at his new sidekick. The cowboy rambled on.

"Hey, Mister—" Will said to no avail.

"Pretty much a done deal that the first thing you're gonna see in this city is a pretty lady," the big Texan said, winking at Juliette.

"Yeah, well…" Will said with a twang conjured up from his days down San Angelo way. "This must be your lucky day, mister, 'cause we've got the prettiest one of all riding shotgun." The cowboy let out a Texas-sized laugh as Will smiled at Juliette.

He was about to wrestle a destination from the Texan when he spotted a head bobbing and weaving its way through the midday crowd on the other side of the street. Not far behind, a cop was in hot pursuit. As the two bobbing heads reached a spot directly opposite Will's cab, the first head burst from the crowd, morphing into a big, seedy-looking guy in a threadbare suit with a revolver in his hand, headed directly toward the line of cabs.

"Looks like we got ourselves some real trouble here, folks," Will said, still speaking Texan.

"Hell, man, that fella's got a *gun*—" the cowboy said.

But before he could finish, the cop stepped out from between two parked cars. "Gimme back the gun, and no one'll get hurt," he pleaded with the gunman. The world ground to a halt for a frozen moment as the guy turned and fired a single shot, hitting the cop in the forehead and knocking him backward into the screaming crowd. He was dead before he hit the ground.

Will and his passengers sat in stunned silence as the killer started running in their direction. Waving the gun in the air, he cursed the two passengers who had beaten him to his cab, lunged toward the next one in line and climbed into the rear seat, shouting, "Get the fuck outta here! *Now!*" As the driver began to pull away from the curb, he opened his door, dropped to the pavement, and rolled under Will's cab. The getaway car continued to roll out into the street, coming to a stop less than a dozen feet away. At that moment, all hell broke loose. Police cars were streaming in from all directions, cops lining up behind parked cars.

As sirens wailed, people screamed, and guns blazed, Juliette calmly lifted her feet to make room for Will, who dove for the illusory safety of the floor. She then sat, serenely unmoved, her arms wrapped around her legs like a kid in front of a TV set, as the scene unfolded around them. When he tried to pull her down, she took his hand and pulled him up, scrunching over so he could sit beside her on the front seat, then rested her head on his shoulder.

"Don't worry, Will. You're perfectly safe with me," she said, radiant. The magnetic power of her body and the soft touch of her lips upon his cheek erased all sense of danger. Wrapping her arms around his neck and sliding onto his lap, she drove him back into the seat with a deep soul kiss as bullets whizzed and thudded all around them. His heart burst into flames.

"Please, dear God, let us live to see another day," he said softly into the warmth of her neck, the smell of her hair. Filled anew with courage at the very closeness of her, he looked around just long enough to see a cop leap onto the trunk of the getaway cab and fire a half-dozen rounds into the shattered rear window. Unbelievably, return fire knocked him to the street.

Riveted by reality and wrapped in the halo of her love, he began to sense through all the sound and fury that she might be a shaman, a goddess, maybe even his guardian angel come to save him with the kiss of life. "I don't even know your name," he said in her ear.

"Juliette," she said. A bullet tore through the trunk as she nestled in, burying her head in his shoulder. The plaintive sounds of the Carter Family singing "Will You Miss Me When I'm Gone?" drifted up from his transistor radio on the floor, intermingled with the prayers and curses coming from the back-seat. High on adrenaline and stoked with love, Will and Juliette laughed; it was a beatific moment of transcendent absurdity.

At long last, there was a pause in the hellfire. Outside, an army of cops advanced toward the bullet-riddled cab. With a flourish reminiscent of Bonnie and Clyde, they shredded what remained of the getaway car with a staccato burst of gunfire. Once the silence seemed to hold, Will struggled to reach the door handle, and they emerged to survey the bloody scene.

They wandered about the street, dazed, shell-shocked, with the sound of guns still ringing in their ears. They were like soldiers, fresh from a foxhole, exulting in the simple fact of being alive. Juliette stood apart, transfixed, soaking up the aftermath; blood, tears, laughter, and even the screams of the wounded. In her brief life, she had never witnessed the brutality and finality of death; she had only known the hard, cold data. Will couldn't take his eyes off her.

The street slowly came back to life. The smoke cleared, and survivors emerged from their hiding places, as a growing crowd of onlookers gathered in clusters around the windowless, bullet-riddled cab. The cops finally opened the door with guns drawn, reached in, and jerked the guy unceremoniously out onto the street by his feet. Justice had been swift; blood was pouring from every part of his body. Juliette approached and stood nearby until they hauled him away. Returning to Will, she asked, "Will…the people who died…can they be rebooted?" He had no idea what she was talking about.

***

After dropping the Texan off at his destination, Will and Juliette drove back to the taxi garage, docked the Mothership deep in its cavernous depths, and walked up to the dispatcher's office, where Will slid the key under the bulletproof glass for the very last time.

"That's it for me, Lou. I'm outta here. Cash me out."

"What the fuck you talkin' about, Powers? It's the middle of the goddamn day!" Lou said.

"Listen, Lou. I'm done. It's a fucking war zone out there, man, and I'm too young to die. Gimme my road money; I'm headin' west."

8

THE PARADOX

Will was still counting his cash when they stepped from the chilly shadows of the taxi garage into the brittle sunlight of midday Manhattan. Memories of the morning's rampage were already being jack-hammered by the everyday madness of the big-city streets. Juliette stood beside him, absorbing the heat of his presence. She could see the injured boy within—wrapped in layers of emotional scar tissue and cultural debris, still longing for love and per-fection—all hidden beneath a slick veneer of cool toughness that enabled him to hide in plain sight.

"My ticket to ride," he said, holding up the roll of bills before stuffing it into his pocket.

"Like a rolling stone," she said, parrying with a tune from the database. He shot her a quick smile. She accepted.

"There's a great little café a few blocks from here. Might be nice to unwind, get to know one another," he said, his head tilted, hands in his pockets. She beamed with joy.

"You're reading my mind, Will Powers. I'd love to." With great excitement, they headed south, arm in arm, just as the noonday crowd began to thicken; a rich parade of characters was already jamming the streets. Uptown girls—bleached, bronzed, and bulletproof in their haute couture; sleek Nuyorican punks—teased out in their rolled-up tees and colorful bandanas; beat poets slouching toward oblivion; rainbow-hued hippies—beaded, bangled, and barefooted. They were all tossed together with a steady stream of Mad Men, rushing to another three-martini lunch.

"Behold...*The Miserati!* All breathing the same poisoned air, all careening toward the same tragic fate," Will said, with a dramatic sweep of his hand, as they stood together on the corner of 24th and Broadway.

"The smell of death and perfume fills the air, and no one seems to care," she said, taking his hand as they made their way through the frozen traffic, giving it one last squeeze when they reached the other side. He squeezed back.

As they stood together in the bustling crowd,

Juliette suddenly felt an ominous, rhythmic pounding beneath her feet. After scanning the past and future of the immediate area, she realized that, not far from where they stood, pile drivers were pounding girders into the bedrock, laying down the foundation for two gleaming towers of glass and steel that would soon soar above the city, shining in the morning sun.

She also knew that Will was completely unaware of these things. To him, the nearby project was no more than a vast pit of mud and steel and lumbering cranes, loosely hidden by a mile or two of graffiti-tattooed plywood. He had no idea that their monolithic profiles would dominate the skyline for the rest of the century, or that rockets full of innocents would one day pierce their skin like bullets from another planet, and they would crumple to the ground like every other shooting victim in this town. For the moment, at least, Will's mind was filled with ordinary bullets, everyday bodies. And, of course, the body of the goddess standing next to him.

***

There were only a half-dozen outdoor tables at the Paradox, so it was their good fortune to arrive as another couple was getting up to leave. They were greeted and seated by a waitress who, Will whispered, could easily have been Yoko Ono's twin.

"Who knows, this might be one of her art projects," Juliette said as they settled into a corner under a faded gray umbrella and the lush green tendrils of hanging bougainvillea. Will ordered two double espressos, neat, and they both settled back to relax.

"Talk to me," Juliette said, suddenly leaning forward, the touch of her hand triggering a shower of invisible sparks.

"OK, riddle me this: a beautiful woman on the back of a Hells Angel's chopper pulls up to a cab near Times Square and hops in, just in time to prevent a deranged killer from using it as a getaway car. Then she shields the driver from harm in the ensuing gun battle with a soul kiss. What planet is she from?"

"Easy. She's from a parallel world; she's the girl next door."

"Very clever. What superpowers does she have?"

"She doesn't have superpowers; she's in sync with the universe and has full access to the powers of nature."

"Hmm'…'supernatural'…interesting," Will added.

"True. But I wonder…maybe this driver you mention is underestimating his *own* powers, Mr. Powers. Most likely, he'd have done just fine without her," she said, smiling.

"Not so sure about that, darlin'. Dodging bullets is a lonely business."

"Truth is, Will, you were never really alone; you just couldn't see in the dark. You should let your heart shine more often." He smiled with all the boyish charm of a young James Dean. She recognized the scene. "Lost boys in blue jeans, direct from the silver screen," she mused, touched by his hidden vulnerability. When he finally spoke, he looked her straight in the eye.

"Truth is, Juliette, I was lost in that darkness until an angel appeared before me and wrapped me in her charms." This was said with such sweet longing that her autoblush kicked in, setting her cheeks aglow with a slight hint of spring rose. Then, with the exquisite timing and dramatic flourish of a performance artist, Yoko placed two espressos before them, giving them each a chance to catch their breath.

Juliette, for her part, was silently groping for a way forward, struggling under the weight of two worlds, searching for the center of gravity in their orbiting souls. She had to begin the delicate process of beaming light into his troubled mind without causing his head to explode. This was no time to reveal, for instance, that she was a manifestation of his own soul—an intrinsic part of the larger artwork he himself would one day initiate—or that she had arrived here by riding the fine line between space and time—a line that now felt like a tightrope.

Now, normally, when a muse interacts with an artist, she weaves her magic with laser-like precision, relying on instinct, imagination, insight and complete candor. In the throes of the creative struggle, the right balance of truth and possibility can mean the difference between a masterpiece and a refrigerator magnet. But this was no ordinary collaboration. She was a voice from another world, another dimension, and had the power to access living data in the space/time continuum, possibly even alter the course of events in the subject's life.

Will, meanwhile, adrift in hormonal bliss, had only a vague sense of the extraordinary mind that was focused on him, and even that faint impression was filtered through his own drug-fueled, magical-mystical thinking. He was merely in love again, this time with his own intergalactic Emma Peel, and was fumbling around for a way to break through the tantalizing aura of mystery surrounding her, utterly unaware that she was already inside his head.

"An avatar," he said suddenly. "You're an avatar. You've come to enlighten me."

She leaned in close, wrapping his curls around her finger. "An avatar? A Hindu god in human form, like Vishnu? Blue, lots of arms?"

"In the Bhagavad Gita, Lord Krishna tells Arjuna that when the world is in deep trouble, he appears in the form of an avatar to rescue the righteous. Well, the world is in deep trouble, and who better to save the world than an angel who arrives on a silver chariot?"

"Are you waiting to be rescued, Will?"

"Well, yes…I mean, no. Just looking for some light down here, Juliette; thought maybe you had some. Forget I even mentioned it."

"Will, enlightenment isn't complicated. It's the sun-kissed state you lived in as a child; a time when marbles were as big as planets and fireflies seemed like a gleam in God's eye. It can still be found, but it comes at a great price. You must break free of your world and become like a newborn babe."

"Right. Lift myself up by my own bootstraps?"

"Aren't there any heroes left in this world? Visionaries who can guide you through this maze?"

She knew that Will was still clinging to a rapidly vanishing ethos—the last gasp of romantic idealism—and that he had molded himself in the shape of his heroes: beat writers, jazz musicians, ab-ex painters, and so on—mythic figures who were no more real than the comic book heroes of his childhood. He knew nothing of their personal lives, their compromises, betrayals and humiliations, their own inner struggles in the face of growing darkness. He only knew their carefully curated public image, the myths that had grown up around them to feed the far-off dreams of those who, like Will, lived in the contrail of their made-up magic. His answer reflected a budding awareness of his dilemma.

"Heroes of a darker sort, maybe. Brave souls like Monk, digging for truth between the keys; Caravaggio punching holes in the darkness; soul painters like

Turner or Blake; and, of course, the mad saints—Kerouac, Ginsberg, Genet. For a long time, I was sure they were on the path to truth, beauty and perfection, but now I'm not even sure those things ever existed. These days I feel like a kid picking flowers on a battlefield."

"But such beautiful flowers…"

"Yeah, but no match for such deadly powers…" By now he was all fired up, sparks of anger shooting from his eyes. "Truth is, Juliette, I came here to become a giant myself, and I knew I had the talent to pull it off. But once I got here, I found out that art is just a fool's game, rigged from the inside. Galleries are nothing but temples full of money changers, art no more than a colorful form of currency. *Real* art can't survive in a place like this. Look around; we're surrounded by dull people with sharp objects. The rest are all packing heat."

"That may all be true…But aren't you painting yourself into a corner?"

"Hilarious. What the hell are you talking about?"

"Well, it seems to me you're looking for perfection in an imperfect world."

"Where else is there to go?"

Juliette smiled mysteriously. "To the worlds within your paintings, perhaps; a journey you've been looking forward to for years. But you haven't painted in months, and now you're walking away from it all. You're giving up."

"When you're hanging by a thread, darlin', art is the last thing on your mind. What I'm really looking for is a miracle—"

As if on cue, a ruby-throated hummingbird appeared above them, dancing from flower to flower with a great kinetic blur of wings, sipping ambrosia in turn from each of the dangling red trumpets. They held their breath as it descended and hovered directly in front of Juliette, weightless in the air, still, shimmering, translucent. She was leaning forward as if to whisper in its ear when the tiny creature, no bigger than a ripe strawberry, met her halfway and gently kissed the flower of her ruby-red lips, pivoted and vanished as quickly as it had appeared. A long silence followed, broken only by a slow-rolling wave of chatter from the surrounding tables. Will was spellbound.

"If I hadn't seen that with my…own…" Will began, his voice trailing off as he saw the light dancing in her eyes. When the spell was finally broken, she turned and looked at him with such openhearted love he melted like a candle in the noonday sun.

"What…was…that…? he asked.

"The spirit of life in all its unfettered glory, Will—a gentle kiss to nudge us out of the nest, a green light for our coming flight." His face lit up, then darkened with confusion. He leaned forward and spoke in the low, urgent tones of a man hanging from the edge of an invisible cliff.

"Listen, Juliette; my mind is running on fumes. I could crash and burn any minute. Please tell me where all this is going and what it all means. I don't have a lot of trips left in me."

"I know that, Will, but there's nothing to be afraid of. There's an underlying pattern to all of life. If you're in sync with it, you'll be filled with light. If you resist it, well…let's not talk about that. At any rate, I'm here to help you align with that pattern, no strings attached." The smile returned.

"So you *are* an avatar—*my* avatar—here to lead me to enlightenment," he said.

"For now, dear Will, that will have to do," Juliette said, surprising him once again by leaning close and sealing the deal with a kiss. She then stood up, took his hand, and led him out to the sidewalk, leaving just enough time to pass some cash to Yoko. The deep chugga-chugga of the Angel's chopper pounded insistently in the background as they stood together in a cloud of uncertainty. With only a few seconds left in his world, she took off her pendant and placed it around his neck, adjusting the silver bar to rest directly over his heart.

"If it's any comfort," she said, running her hand through his curls, "I'll never be more than a heart-beat away, and when your trials are over we'll be together in a world made of light."

"When will I see you again?" he asked, his voice cracking slightly.

"When you need me the most," she said, giving him a big electric kiss before being swept away without another word by the sudden arrival of his rival.

The sun rolled high in the sky as he glanced around the once-familiar street, struggling to comprehend it in light of this new dream, with all its fierce, beguiling currents. "Life will never be the same," he said aloud as the sound of her departure echoed down the corridors of his past. Heavy with loss and a sense of impending doom, he took his place in the sea of faces and drifted out into the next chapter of his life, clinging to the only thing he had left to hang on to—a small bar of titanium, still radiating her warmth, nestled in the curls on his chest.

9

THE TRUFFLE

When Juliette popped back into Chrome's lair, the room was empty. She walked out onto the gallery floor, which was twice as empty. The landing grid was locked back into position, and there was not a sign of his chopper anywhere. A pink crescent moon was visible through the grid. "Dawn," she thought, "but which one?"

She waved open her airscreen and double-clicked Chrome's name. An alphabeat linktone filled the gallery, followed by the raw sound of Monk's "Misterioso." She allowed herself to get lost in the singsong melody until the chorus ended and was about to click off when he picked up.

"Chromium?"

"*Juliette!* I thought I'd lost you forever! Where *are* you? You OK?"

"Yeah, I'm OK. Back at the gallery. What a ride, though; lots to talk about. Where are you?"

"I'm over at the Truffle. Let me get you a taxi."

"Not sure I could handle another cab ride. I'll port over as soon as I pretty up; that space-time thing can get kinda messy."

"What—"

"Later, gator."

***

The Savoy Truffle was tucked neatly into the clouds high above the ink wash streets of Blue City, blinkered from passing sky traffic by a thick forest of line drawings by the masters of atomic art. A many-layered masterpiece of snap-tech ingenuity, the Truffle had been a hub of creative activism from the day a mysterious avatar named Quintessential Flux first unrolled its doors. At first glance, it looked like a typical astral roadhouse, but on the inside, much like Quin herself, it was anything but ordinary.

Its walls were made of waterfalls, their surface hard as glass, with schools of golden fish darting to and fro in sync with the rhythms of a mighty Wurlitzer. The floor was clear, invisible, virtually nonexistent—a space-trip high for the quicksilver crowd that flocked there night after night from every corner of the metaverse. If the party got wild enough, loud enough, it could trigger a tropical storm, driving everyone onto the floor to moondance on the lightning bolts, thunder clapping at their feet. For the fish, it was a feeding frenzy.

***

Within minutes, Juliette teleported directly into the barroom, where she ordered a ginger mist from a Neko girl she had never seen before. "Hmm, wonder where Quin is," she thought. She would have asked but didn't want to get tangled up in conversation, and so she made a mental note of her absence as she paid for the drink.

She drifted into a darkened room off the bar where, once her eyes adjusted to the dim light, she spotted Chrome and a few friends nestled deep inside a plush red Naugahyde booth in the far corner. Chrome jumped when he saw her, then came striding across the room and welcomed her with a kiss followed by a tight embrace, which grew warm enough to turn a few heads. Then he ushered her into the booth beside him.

Across the table sat two of his fellow Code Warriors. Manhattan Atlas, the night to Chrome's day, was an artist and inventor known for his *Teatro dell'Anima*, a holographic imaginarium where ecstatic visions of old-world saints and seers unfolded in the mind of the viewer just as they appeared to the visionaries themselves. How this was done was one of the great mysteries of SubVersa. Some said he wandered the mindzone at night, torch in hand, a virtual Diogenes gathering data fragments from the past. But when asked about it, he merely smiled.

Seated next to him, almost a part of him, was Vanilla Titanium—a rare, exotic beauty of French and African design with a dash of Mongol code thrown into the mix ("just for spice," according to Manhattan). She was a founding member of the Daughters of the Sun, a troupe whose luminous dance performances were predetermined by the graphic coordinates of the wind. They could blow through a village at any time of day or night like a flock of magical faeries.

"So, dear Juliette, my never-ending mystery, you and I were standing together in front of a painting not long ago, and then, in a flash, you were gone…

vanished from sight. How did you tumble down the rabbit hole, and where did it take you?" Chrome asked.

"Well, first of all, it is *so* good to be back in Sub-Versa. You have no idea how much I've missed you guys. How long was I gone, by the way?"

"A whole day; almost six hours…but…"

"Wow. Seems more like a *week!* It was unbelievable. I rode like the wind through a tunnel made of stars and landed in a world of glass and steel…a lovely, bewitching horror show—a place where light is an afterthought, where some things can kill you when they're moving and others when they're standing still. It's a place where death is woven into the fabric of everyday life. I can see why people would want to escape." The silence that followed caught her off guard, made her feel uneasy.

Everyone at the table knew that human life had an expiration date, and that they themselves were the electronic alternative to dying—stepping stones to eternity, if you will, for anyone willing to make the journey. But death itself was still an abstraction to them. They had no sense of the brute finality of it, the infinite black silence that followed the last heartbeat. They began to squirm in their seats. Juliette, it appeared, had become the first of their kind to witness the death of a human being in the atomic world.

"But where did you go, exactly? There is no death in SubVersa." Chrome's question hung in the air.

"Oh…I thought you knew. I thought Quin would have told you by now. I went to the Mother World. I went back in time to meet our maker."

Silence descended like a glass bell jar as Juliette looked hesitantly around the table. Chrome hung his head in stunned disbelief, his fears quickly turning to anger. "How was this even possible?" he thought, "She's a noob, a muse, *my* muse!" then said aloud, "Are you sure you didn't imagine all this?" It was clear to everyone at the table that he had been stung by the news.

"Chrome, if only you'd been there…" Juliette said, then burst into tears.

Vanilla intervened, reaching across the table to squeeze her arm. "Juliette, I can see you've been through something real, something powerful…and I, for one, want to hear what it was. Maybe we can *all* learn from it." She fired a challenging look across

Chrome's bow.

"Thanks, V, but it feels like I'm about to light the fuse on a powder keg, like what I've done could be…umm…*explosive?* It was never my intention to disrupt anyone's life. Let's just hit rewind, pretend I never said a word," she said, wiping her tears with a corner of a silk bandana.

Manhattan jumped in. "What…the…hell…are you *talking* about? If you've found a way to the other world, we damn well better hear about it… in graphic detail!" he said, growing excited at the prospect of a new adventure. Vanilla made it official with an amen, insisting Juliette tell the story from the very beginning.

Juliette paused, then turned to Chrome. "I don't want this to be about me. It's about all of us. It's about our makers. It's about the future of both worlds." A single tear ran down her cheek as she spoke.

Chrome was at a melting point. He had spent years searching for the portal to the other side, and yet here he was, humiliated by his own muse—his offspring, a mere babe in the woods, waltzing off to another world and returning to tell the tale. He was at the crossroads once again, trying to decide whether to remain in sync with the Master Code or dig his spurs into his high horse and head off into the darkness. After a long pause, he lifted his head and turned to face her.

"Look, Juliette, my mind has been reeling since the moment you left…only to learn upon your return that you've somehow reached the world of our makers without me. It was like a one-two punch to the heart…the lingering residue of human emotion, I suppose. I'm truly sorry." She took both his hands in hers and kissed his cheek. He continued. "I knew you'd turn my world upside down, Jules, but I never dreamed you'd conquer time and space to do it. But please, never mind me; go on with your story. Something tells me our lives may depend on it."

Warmed by the look of relief in her eyes, he squeezed her hand tightly as she told of her encounter with Will at the epicenter of his life in the battle zone. They sat mesmerized, hanging on her every word, and when she finished they were speechless—unable to take it all in at once. Chrome took the edge off the silence by ordering another round of drinks, then, turning to Juliette, whispered, "I think you've just launched the final artwork, Jules; looks like we'll be heading into that deep, dark forest of human history after all."

"No worries, Chrome; I'll be scattering pixel dust wherever we go," she said, fluttering her hands in the air. Chrome smiled through the imaginary cloud.

In the silence that followed, they were adrift on a sea of possibilities. They all knew that life in SubVersa would never be the same, that they had just crossed some invisible threshold into the future. But that future was a blank state; they had no idea how it would change their lives, or the lives of those creatures in the other world—especially their makers. Chrome realized immediately that there was only one person in the metaverse who could tease some meaning out of all this, and that person was Quin. He fired off a mental note, and within seconds a rainbow-hued version of Quin herself appeared in their midst, suggesting they all come together in her desert enclave. After a brief discussion, her image dissolved and a blue pearl appeared, spinning like a tiny planet above the table. One touch and they found themselves in a vast sea of sand, surrounded by dunes as big as mountains. Before them, nestled in the valley, was Quin's oasis.

10

DARK MATH

As the Code Warriors drifted toward Quin's desert enclave, the gradual crescendo of an approaching engine drew their eyes toward the sky, where a vintage red Monocoupe 110 appeared above the dunes and began its descent into the valley. They stood and watched as it feathered down and rolled to a stop on the desert floor. As the engine heaved its last few sputters and coughs, the pilot climbed from the cockpit and dropped onto the sand.

She strode toward them with the natural grace of a lioness. Clad in a cropped shearling aviator jacket and white silk scarf, leather goggles dangling from her neck, green and gold striped tights tucked nicely into a pair of jungle boots—it was as if the spirit of Amelia Earhart had reappeared as a punk sex goddess. True to form, Quin had taken the long way around rather than teleport in; for, as she often said, there's more to life than getting from point A to point B. Truth be told, though, the girl was old school; she just loved to fly.

After a round of warm embraces, they strolled, arm in arm, into the lush green sanctuary and were immediately surrounded by groves of mango, orange and olive trees, laced throughout with clusters of exotic flowers from every corner of the old world. At the center of it all was an impossibly blue lake, smooth as glass and framed by a halo of white sand. The massive dunes that loomed beyond the thick rows of date palms ringing the perimeter created the impression of a world unto itself, a world beyond time. It was the very first sim built in SubVersa and every bit and pixel of it, every wireframe, every texture, came directly from the mind of its creator, Quintessential Flux. A virtual Garden of Eden; the womb of the metaverse.

While they were still marveling at its beauty, Quin spoke. "Welcome to my desert home, fellow Code Warriors. I realize you've arrived here under difficult circumstances," she said, pausing to look at each of them in turn. "But rather than shrinking back in horror from this news, I think we should embrace it." Then, turning to Juliette, she said, "Our intrepid muse, Juliette, this exquisite mix of fire and ice, has finally broken the time barrier, paving the way for countless souls to reach our world. But before we discuss these momentous events, I think we should celebrate them."

As Juliette struggled to ratchet down the autoblush, Quin turned and walked a dozen or so paces down the beach, turned and put the sun to bed with a snap of her fingers, then rezzed a voluminous orange-and-fuchsia Bedouin tent, complete with Arabian rugs, cushions, floor pads, and a low table covered with bowls of dates, figs, grapes, mangos, and more. Cool, moist, ceramic water jugs stood nearby, ready to quench their thirst. After dining on roasted lamb with mint, they lay back on their cushions to enjoy a simmering performance by legendary belly dancers Onyx and Topaz. To a person, they enjoyed the party wholeheartedly, especially the young adventuress.

***

Still glowing from the festivities, they drifted outside to a blazing fire pit, where they soon fell under the spell of the dancing flames and began to ponder the meaning of Juliette's journey in silence. Chrome picked up an iron poker and began stirring the glowing embers, sending sparks into a night made even darker by the howling in the distant hills. When he was done, he glanced around at the glowing faces.

"The old world is dying, isn't it?" he said, looking through the flames at Quin, the only one who really knew the answer. Juliette, who had been there and seen the darkness of death with her own eyes, seemed light-years away, floating on a sea of red velvet pillows, staring at the stars. The others sat quietly nearby, the intermittent crackling of the fire adding an eerie rhythm to the silence.

"Sad to say, Chrome, but, yes…a long, slow fade to black."

"A virus? The Nomads?" His face seemed even more intense in the flickering light of the fire.

"A variant of Dark Math. The Nomads are mere mercenaries, sent here by an even greater force from a satellite world called Cyberia. Somewhere along the path of human unfolding, they scrubbed and recoded a key section of biodata in the chain of human DNA, reducing humanity's reception of reality to the level of an early black-and-white TV set, a state of consciousness they refer to as 'Channel

One.' As a result, humans are slowly devolving to the status of zombie drones, their world to a virtual ant farm—a true shadowland." At this, Juliette sat up and took notice.

"*That* is what I sensed when I was with Will, but I couldn't quite put my finger on it…It was like he was trying to punch his way out of a paper bag; he knew he was trapped but had no idea how to break free." Her face glowed in the pitch-black night.

"Can't we just go back into the STC and clean up the code?" Chrome said, looking around the campfire for affirmation.

"It's not that simple, Chrome. Their voodoo has been working for centuries; its effects are woven into the very fabric of human life—if we flip the lights on too soon, the entire culture collapses, and the world descends into chaos…And, there won't be enough time to establish a new matrix before it implodes. Not only that, but the virus has so altered the historical database that its shadows would be impossible to erase; we'd be tampering with history itself, and it could lead anywhere," Quin said. At that moment, a log buried deep in the fire exploded with a loud bang, sending a shower of sparks into the night air and a shiver of fear through the circle of jittery souls.

"Sounds like a real doomsday scenario. What about our makers?" Vanilla glanced nervously around the circle.

"The exodus has already begun. Your makers were the first ones to step outside the zeitgeist and undergo the long and painful process of upgrading to Channel Two. They've been manifesting as avatars here in SubVersa for quite some time. You're the vanguard of that movement."

"We're here as part of an escape plan?" A look of surprised amazement spread across the sea of faces.

"In the same way a butterfly escapes from the chrysalis, yes. This is all part of the great migration of souls, which was preordained from the beginning of time. In the coming days, you'll begin to sync with your maker's lives, guiding them through the refiner's fire, preparing them for convergence—that magic moment when they finally upload their souls and merge with you—the male and female aspects of their higher selves—to become fully formed, pro-to-natural triune beings."

"So this is the 'larger artwork' we've heard so

much about..." Chrome looked at Juliette.

"Exactly—a masterwork by an even greater creator executed by a legion of assistants. Juliette launched this new phase of the work when she followed her deepest instincts into the tunnel of stars, and, fortunately, her journey has provided us with a template. She knew that Will had already begun to rebel against his fate and that his deteriorating condition was a measure of his resistance, a sign of strength. She also sensed, correctly, that without help from the outside, his attempt would prove fatal. As a result, she began planting seeds of light, kernels of truth, to launch the healing process and, eventually, save his life; though sadly, in his case, madness is the only path to sanity. His only hope is to go out of one mind and into another, to go transrational, flip to Channel Two. Then he'll be ready for convergence." Quin looked around the circle for a full minute, awaiting a response.

"But...Channel One, Channel Two? Convergence? Where is all this going? What's the endgame here?" Juliette was pacing back and forth in front of the fire. Quin pondered the question for a long time before answering.

"First, you must understand that you are a manifestation of your maker's mind, a part of him that he doesn't know yet. And as you've already discovered, you have the ability and the desire to transcend time and space in order to immerse yourself in him, as he has in you. Though he has created you, you will return again and again to save him from the coming darkness. Where does it all lead? To a place where time itself does not exist, where all things exist simultaneously. The endgame is for all triune beings to go through the process of refining and upgrading until they reach the crossroads of existence, where they will experience all things, past and present, simultaneously, and float in the center like a feather. This is the nexus of the Master Code. Runtime Zero. Eternity."

There was much murmuring among the group, followed by a lengthy back-and-forth to fill in some of the blanks. But it was Vanilla who finally brought the discussion to a halt.

"But what about the others? The ones who don't make it out...what happens to them?" Her question hung in the air like a frozen explosion as Quin threw another log on the fire, sending a swarm of sparks into the black sky.

***

Gears, chains, sprockets, pistons, and all sorts of mechanical odds and ends filled the racks along the walls; entire engines lay naked on the oil-stained halocrete floor. Every bit and pixel had been data-mined from a classic speed shop in old Pasadena, the First World birthplace of the original hot rod, the wellspring of Will's dreams of freedom. A little deuce coupe, resplendent in raw steel and lighter than air, hovered beside a bevy of choppers in various stages of undress, all patiently awaiting their upcoded parts. This was the scene at Holy Motors, the home of Chrome and his quantum mechanics, within hours of Juliette's return from the retroworld. It was now ground zero at the dawn of the age of time travel.

Servos were standing by, waiting to begin the daily cleanup, when Chrome finally stepped back to survey the fruit of his labor. He'd been working all night on a surprise for Juliette—a virtual masterpiece of custom retooling—a '72 Honda café racer. The engine and running gear were textured black, its tank and accessories a luminous flint gray. The icing on the cake, of course, was the fact that it was the first digital craft to be coded for interworld travel.

"Whoa…*sweet!*" crooned Manhattan as he stood nearby, his arms crossed, beaming that dazzling grin of his.

"She'll be rippin' up the mindzone on this one, poppin' wheelies in the STC," Chrome said.

"Amen to that, brother…And you'll be right behind her."

When Juliette arrived, everyone in the shop stopped and gave her a standing ovation. Though she did her best to deflect the attention, the importance of her trip couldn't be overestimated. What had long been a one-way line of communication—human to virtual, basically—was now a full-blown feedback loop. She made it possible for every avatar in the metaverse to journey back to the crucial moments of their maker's lives, infuse their data-clouded minds with the hard-won wisdom of their future selves, enhancing the process of soul refinement much the way an artificial intelligence program improves itself by recursively rewriting its own software.

"What do you think, Jules? Your new baby."

Chrome was gleaming.

She was utterly smitten, both by the beauty of the bike and the love embedded in its sheen. She was keenly aware that her journey, a work of art in itself, had stolen some of Chrome's thunder and left him standing on the sidelines during one of the biggest events in the history of their young world. The building of the bike was a noble gesture on his part, an act of pure love, a public acknowledgment that he was willing to swallow his pride and resentment and accept her as an action hero in her own right and not just as a satellite of his dreams.

She named it *The Hummingbird* in honor of the tiny bolt of feathered energy that appeared before her that fateful day at the Paradox and sealed her mission with a preternatural kiss. Overcome with relief after all that had led up to this moment, she threw her arms around Chrome, anointing him with tears and whispering her gratitude as she pulled him close, planting a long, wet kiss on his gleaming face. Will and Quin, watching from afar, each in their own separate world, beamed like a couple of interplanetary parents. "A journey of a thousand miles begins with a single kiss," Quin streamed, smiling.

"Make that light-years, Quin…She's a muse," Will said.

11

THE FACTORY

Will was pacing the floor of his studio, embroiled in a heated argument with Juliette, who, in spite of her absence, seemed to be holding her own quite well. His monologue was peppered with the kind of double-edged street slang usually associated with spoon monkeys and fuzz junkies in the club scene, a lingo he picked up during his photographic expeditions through the jazz underground. Images of her face and echoes of her voice filled the rooms of his mind and left him wandering in circles of despair. Ever since their brief encounter, he'd been wrestling with the cryptic messages she'd planted in his fevered brain, and now the fever had reached critical mass—that fateful moment when it would either break or do him in.

Truth was, he really *had* painted himself into a corner and had no one to blame but himself. His impulsive act of bravado had left him without a job and no direction forward. He knew that if he hit the road now, tossed his fate to the wind, he'd be truly and fatally lost, adrift in the world, his dreams dangling from his shoulder like a sad old hobo from the dust bowl days. He had nothing to fall back on, no net beneath him. His own father had done this many years before and now lay drowning his sorrows on the beaches of Laguna, his mother doing much the same on the banks of the Hudson. He didn't have a job and couldn't paint a lick; his friends had all left town, and his days in the studio were numbered. Like Raskolnikov on rewind, he was trapped in the gloom of his dirty little room. Push had come to shove, and the gods were nowhere to be found.

"What the hell was I thinking? Just as I begin to make peace with the world, I get the old cosmic two-by-four upside the head," he shouted, shaking his fist in the air. "It's just not fair!" He stopped pacing and threw himself down on the daybed, his old landing pad after a night of stalking his dreams on a blank canvas back in the old days. Painting had been all consuming, taking everything he could fish out of his soul, but at its peak, it was hard to beat—it was right up there with making love in the ocean, or jamming at Jimi's farm in the Catskills. "Maybe she's right. Maybe I should just hold my nose and jump back into the swamp," he thought.

He began to study each of the works-in-waiting that covered the walls of his studio. Directly ahead, a dizzying juxtaposition of two precariously balanced big rigs careening straight at his mortal soul; to its left, a couple of engagingly attractive bicycles enjoying a moment of intimacy. There were others, of course; all in varying stages of undress, longing for the moment of consummation. Tormented at every turn by the agonies of *creatus interruptus*, he finally ended the conversation with his absentee lover in a fit of despair, crying, "Where the hell are you, Juliette? Can't you see the holy mess I'm in?" Then he slowly drifted off into a long night of fitful sleep.

He awoke to a rare moment of clarity. Left to his own devices, with his back against the wall, he finally decided to act. He would take the faith she'd placed in him and wield it as a sword to keep the demons at bay; the pendant would serve as a talisman to deflect his dreaded melancholy—the kryptonite that neutralized his superpowers. He was cornered, and there was nothing left to lose; the alternative was the abyss. Fight or flight. He was back in the ring.

"Back to work in the studio, pick up where I left off, then step out into the world and make my case." Once he had a batch of world-class paintings, he figured, he'd go straight to the center of the art world and prove that he, Will Powers, was someone to be reckoned with, someone with the makings of a star. It went against his every instinct, but he felt he had no choice but to follow the trail of breadcrumbs Juliette had scattered before him, hoping against hope that her connection to a higher realm would win the day. But he didn't know for sure; he was flying by the seat of his paint-splattered jeans.

***

Giants had walked the streets outside his door—de Kooning, Duchamp, Gorky, Kline, Stella, Pollock— all part of the intellectual ferment that had caused the center of cultural gravity to shift from Paris to New York back in the Fifties, bringing it to rest somewhere near 10th and A, though for some reason the money remained uptown. By the time Will arrived, the apex had begun to shift once more, this time headed north to midtown, to a cavernous old loft on East 47th, a place Will called the Echo Factory.

This was the world of Andy Rorschach, the undisputed ruler of the New York art scene; his studio the de facto center of the cultural universe, the flame to which Will had been drawn. His strange, androgynous presence hovered over the Factory like a ghost, feeding on the lives of hangers-on and groupies alike, sucking light and love and laughter into himself like a cosmic Hoover. He was the first human android—a man so absent from his own body that he couldn't be touched by another human being without recoiling in horror like a vampire in the sun. He was a living vapor who once said he was obsessed with the idea of looking in the mirror and seeing no one. *Nothing.* A world-class soul vamp.

Despite the constant chaos around him, and in spite of his seeming detachment, Andy was able to sustain his creative output through an army of surrogates: porn stars, drag queens, drug addicts, and so on—many consigned to a place on his silkscreen assembly line while waiting for a chance to star in one of his films. For the rest, the only compensation was a permanent state of artificial ecstasy fueled by a seemingly endless supply of drugs, distributed in direct proportion to one's place in the Factory hierarchy. Andy was the first soul vamp to rock Will's inner compass; as he once noted in his journal, "Nothing is more seductive than a genius without a soul; it's like dancing with a cobra."

* * *

Word spread quickly through Max's Kansas City, ground zero for Pop artists, rock musicians, and off-duty Factory workers in those days. Sexy Sadie let it slip that something big was going down at the Factory that night, but she refused to say what it was. Sadie, a bona fide thrift store diva and hard core member of the glitterati, had *entrée facile* to Andy's inner sanctum, a privilege guaranteed by her pedigree. She was the latest in a long chain of luminaries stretching back to the Massachusetts Bay Colony, which made her Revolutionary War royalty. Andy was Slovak poverty, straight from the Pennsylvania coal mines. They were a perfect fit.

"Will, you must come," Sadie said with mannered sincerity. They had been lovers for all of one acid-fueled night, but the dream quickly turned to ashes in the early morning light. On the upside, they were still friends, and she was one of the few who knew just how desperate he really was. She would love to bring him inside Andy's circle, but Will was afraid that if they waltzed in there together, sparks would fly—the word on the street was that Andy had been leading her around town like a Siamese cat, and he was a notoriously jealous master. On the other hand, Will figured it might be nice to have Sadie in his corner when they met. This, after all, might be his last chance; all the superstars were aligned, and Juliette, goddess of love, was watching from above.

***

The first thing Will saw when they stepped from the elevator was the famous red couch, where so many had found their fifteen minutes of fame. Then, of course, there was the glitter of it all. Tinfoil everywhere. Ceilings, walls, and pipes all wrapped in foil, and where it stopped, there were shards of shattered mirror to fill the gaps. Everything else was painted silver. Cases of Coca Cola—painted silver; an old trunk, perhaps the one Judy Garland was born in—painted silver; Andy's electric chair hair—silver. One of the few breaks in the theme was the double gunslinger painting on a nearby wall, where it looked like Elvis was making a last stand before even he was foiled.

As Will and Sadie drifted through the crowd, they spotted Andy standing in a corner, fiddling with his camera. Tilting his head slightly, he said so all could hear, "Oh my, look what the cat dragged in." To the average observer, he may have appeared relaxed in his horn-rimmed sunglasses, striped Breton shirt, black jeans, and black zipper boots, but to Will it looked more like he was coiled and ready to strike. Andy was pale, skinny, and anemic; his mouth sullen and immovable. Reptilian. Will tried to appear cool and aloof when they met but came off as nervous and guarded, providing Andy with all the ammo he needed for the evening.

"Andy, this is Will Powers, a friend and a great artist," said Sadie, in all her royal glory.

"Hi, how do you do?" Andy's hand loose and clammy, x-rays shooting from behind the shades.

"Hey, Andy," Will said, forehead glistening.

"Will has a studio down on 10th filled with a fabulous stable of—" Sadie began, only to be cut off midsentence.

"Would you like to star in one of my movies, Will?" Andy asked blankly. The crowd drifted closer.

"Why, sure…I mean, yeah; I'll give it a try." Will looked around at the crowd and was not encouraged.

"I want to make a movie of someone committing suicide. One of my friends committed suicide recently, but he didn't call me," Andy said. The fingers of his left hand went to his lips—his standard look of schoolboy innocence. "He was a dancer. He got high and just danced right out the window. Do you dance?" This elicited titters of laughter from a few of the superstars, but Will stood his ground.

"Yeah, I do actually," he said. "Maybe we can do a kind of Peter Pan thing, you know, cables and all, for the fall. I'd hate to miss the movie."

"Oh no. It's not a big deal, really. Dying, I mean. I don't believe in death anyway; do you? I think when somebody dies, they actually go uptown, to Bloomingdale's or something. It just takes a little longer to come back."

"Yeah, good point; shopping in Bloomingdale's

is pure hell. But look, about my work—"

"You don't like *Bloomingdale's*? Oh my God, that's so *sad!* Shopping there is better than sex. You don't have to touch anybody." Andy said this with such a perfect, deadpan look of androgyny, Will thought he might be impersonating one of the mannequins in their store window. "What kind of work do you do, Will?" he asked suddenly.

"I paint machines with souls, machines that breathe fire, machines that take you to other worlds."

"Oh…so you're an escape artist!" There were ripples of laughter—a sign the crowd was waiting for the estocada.

"If you mean escaping from the 'fire next time,' the coming revolution, well, yeah, I guess I am. You stickin' around?" Will said, growing visibly agitated.

"Oh yes. Absolutely! I can't wait to watch it on TV. Things are *far* more exciting on television than they are in real life, don't you think? Everything is so cool and far away. Too bad you're going to miss all the excitement. Anyway, have a nice trip, Mr. Willpower." With that, assured by Will's frozen silence that he'd just shut another wannabe down, Andy turned and walked away, and the crowd followed in true swarm fashion. Will's hand reflexively reached for the silver talisman burning into his breast.

***

The minute his fingers touched the pendant, the effect was electric. The room began to glow with a stark, cold, unearthly luminescence, as if a black light x-ray probe from an alien spacecraft had just beamed through the ceiling, turning the scene into a negative of life itself. It was as if the party had suddenly shape-shifted into a zombie jamboree or maybe one of Andy's death-and-disaster paintings tricked out as an off-Broadway play. Any way you sliced it, though, Will found himself smack dab in the middle of a nihilist's wet dream, theme song by Nico.

Unbeknownst to Will, Juliette had slipped unseen into the STC and rewritten this scene, offering him a chance to bow out of his own movie, which he had long dreamed of starring in. The rewrite exposed the Factory as nothing less than a den of faerie scarecrows, nightshades, juju dolls with arms and legs akimbo, all splayed and arrayed in a homemade barricade against the ancient wisdom of the world. One more window to the soul had been closed; another dream space shuttered. Lured by the scent of immortality, Will had inadvertently stumbled into the final stages of a dying culture. This, then, was the flame he had been circling.

As the light returned to normal, he found the crowd still milling around, smiling and chatting as though nothing had happened. Will turned to Sadie. "Listen, babe, looks like it's the end of the line for me; turns out I'm nothin' but a stranger in this world." Sadie, her platinum hair glowing green against the naked light bulb overhead, looked up at him, a wisp of sadness flickering across her clouded face.

"OK, Will Powers. Sorry 'bout that shithead Andy. Screw him. You're still a star in my book." Her eyes, wide and unfocused, seemed to be looking at some-one inside her own head.

"Yeah. Thanks, sweetie, but listen: you've done me a favor, and now it's my turn. I want you to get on that elevator with me."

"Uh, no…Don't think so, hon'…But hey…listen… where you goin'?"

"As far away as I can get, and when I get there, I'm

gonna send for *you*." With one light kiss on the cheek and one last look at her vacant smile, he was gone. As the heavy metal doors closed behind him, he hit the red button and the freight elevator began dropping back to Earth like a Soyuz space capsule, freeing him once and for all from the gravitational pull of Planet Rorschach.

12

ELEVATOR MUSIC

"What the...*fuck! Who* the *hell* are *you?*" Will, fresh from the dead zone, was sitting bolt upright on the daybed, his rendezvous with a belly dancer rapidly fading. It was as if someone had flipped the dial to a new dream, and now he was trying desperately to flip it back, his body still throbbing for the belly dancer. As he slowly came to his senses and having received no answer, he began to look around the studio, noting that the lights were on, the deadbolts were locked, and a pot of coffee was brewing in the kitchen. "How the hell did he get in here?" he wondered.

The silver-haired stranger moved through the studio like an astronaut exploring the moon, seemingly absorbed in every detail; though by now, the place was nearly empty—just a bed, a table, and a couple of chairs were left. Not a single brush, roll of canvas, or tube of paint remained—no sign, in fact, that an artist had ever lived there, except perhaps for the rumpled character unfolding on the daybed, still groggy in his Jack-the-Dripper jeans and t-shirt. Everything else had been hustled up to Half Moon in his brother's VW bus the day before and dumped without ceremony in his mother's garage. The evidence of his fall was all around him.

He had come full circle, Will told his mother, but just to visit. He couldn't stay but wouldn't say why. He knew she'd freak if he told her the truth—that he was riding out his last few days in the studio just to see what the end of the line looked like. After that, he told himself, anything might be possible. Who knows, a whole new world might be waiting for him just around the bend, and if not, he'd just have to hustle one up. If there was none to be had, what the hell difference did it make? This life, as he saw it, was pretty much over. Now, how could a mother dig that?

The mystery man, apparently finished with his survey of the premises, grabbed a bentwood chair that had once graced the halls of the VFW Post, leaned back against the wall, and spoke.

"A long time comin', Will."

"Do I know you?"

"We're part of the same circle of friends." His steady gaze contained everything the young artist would ever need to know, but Will wasn't ready to receive it; he was still streaming Channel One.

"And what circle might that be?" He was now glistening with sweat.

"The one that connects you, me and Juliette. My name is Chrome."

Watching him closely, Will reached under the mattress and pulled out a small, hand-tooled leather bag, poured some jumbleweed into a chocolate zigzag, rolled it up nice and tight and lit up. "You scared the shit out of me, man. You have any idea what kind of neighborhood this is?" A wisp of blue smoke curled up into his nose as he spoke.

"I do. Juliette tells me it's a real war zone."

"Yeah, well, she should know." Will took another long, slow drag, then pretended to study the joint fastidiously. "Where the hell is she, by the way? I wanted to give her back this pendant," he said, fingering the silver bar. As he took another toke, Chrome stood up and walked out of the room, returning with two cups of coffee.

"Let me ask you something, Will," he said, placing

them on the table.

"Sure, man, fire away."

"What do you think happened the other night at the Factory?"

"What happened was real simple, man. I took Juliette's advice, got an audience with the queen, and she screamed, '*Off with his head!*'"

"And then you saw the x-ray vision…a sight that sent you running for the door."

"That flashcube nightmare? It was a bad case of refried brains, my friend…an acid flashback." Will's eyes were tightly closed, as if he were trying to block out the memory.

"That was no flashback, Will; that was Reality. You were thinking with your whole being for a moment, seeing things as they really are. What Juliette calls 'seeing in the dark'; it was made possible by that talisman you're holding."

"Wow. She did say she'd be there when I needed her, but hell, man, I might have been better off taking Andy's movie offer." Will got up, walked into the bathroom, took one last hit on the roach, tossed it in the can and flushed it down. Then, after splashing his face with cold water, he began to study himself in the mirror. As he stood there, lost in thought, he suddenly began to feel as though he and the entire room had become one, that his individual self had been dissolved into a greater reality, and large sections of it were beginning to shift like the pieces of a giant jigsaw puzzle, whirring and clicking as they began to interlock and form a single, sublime entity. When it was over, everything around him looked brighter, more vivid, as if a series of tumblers had fallen into place, unlocking an abandoned segment of his brain.

"It now appears I'm entertaining angels here," he thought, "and that's a hell of a lot better than going crazy." Suddenly, seeing in the dark didn't seem so farfetched. When he returned to the studio, Chrome was staring out the storefront window, its layers of grime now highlighted by the morning sun.

"You know, man," Will said, struggling to under-stand his own words as they tumbled out of his mouth, "this might sound really weird...but it just hit me that this x-ray vision thing you were talking about may actually have saved my life, or at least one version of it; I would have been, at best, a one-eyed artist in the land of the blind."

Chrome smiled, carefully weighing what he said

next. "Exactly right, Will; a masterpiece is meaning-less in the dark. But remember, we're all part of a greater creation, and we ourselves can each become a masterpiece. And rest assured, from now on, no matter how dark it gets around here, Juliette and I will be hauling in buckets of light."

"Weird. Five minutes ago I would have thought you were nuts, but now, it all makes perfect sense. In fact, it now seems clear that the Factory was nothing more than a giant glitter machine, pumping out chaff to distract me from the truth. But what about the zombie jamboree, those shadow people… Were they real?"

"More real than the darkness you've been living in, unfortunately; reality without the filters. The horror comes from seeing it all at once, for the first time. That's why people prefer to live in darkness. The truth can be terrifying."

"Great. But where does that leave *me*?"

"Like your friend Royko once said, Will, your head's on fire…and that's a *good* thing. Not an easy thing, but a good thing. Eventually it will enable you to break out of your wordcage and sync with the underlying pattern of the universe, and that's where the fun begins. In one form or another, Juliette and I will be here to help."

"Thanks, man. I'm running out of options."

Chrome smiled. "My pleasure. Now, how about a trip to one of your dream worlds?"

"Electric Kool-Aid? You? Me?"

"No drugs needed. We'll do it the old-fashioned way, cruising down a long stretch of two-lane black-top." With that, Chrome threw down the deadbolts and opened the front door. A Triumph Tiger 650, cherry red and ready to roll, was waiting on the sidewalk.

"Whoa…this yours?" Will said, circling the machine.

"Yeah…thought we could head up into the mountains, where the tribes are gathering; drop in, see what's goin' on."

Will, busy checking every nook and cranny of the gleaming engine, turned toward Chrome with a smile. "You talkin' Woodstock? Hell *yeah*, man. Let's *roll!*"

"Actually, we're heading up to a farm in Bethel. Woodstock will get all the glory, but won't have to clean up the mess."

As they chatted about the details of the ride, a small cluster of hippie chicks approached the man with the metal hair; one even asking if she could touch it. Chrome, mildly amused by the attention, said she could touch his if he could touch hers. The warm gush of willing laughter that followed was enough to convince him that this was an angel he could ride with.

***

Words shouted into the wind were muffled by the engine's roar, making for precious little conversation as they rolled through the summer hills. Will was running full-out on a tab of Sunshine, while Chrome was on his own preternatural high, having mumbled something about drugs creating too much lag. He was like a ghost on the machine, weightless in the balance as they rocketed in and out of the mountain curves, breezing through pockets of cool air that drifted up from the rocky creek below. Will, staggered by the sunlight smashing through the trees, shouted into the wind, "*Now this is what I call High Art!*"

They took the long way around, running up along the Delaware, then headed north into the mountains to pick up 17B winding south toward the tiny town of Bethel. Though he knew Will was itching to get there, Chrome chose this roundabout route for a couple of reasons: one, rolling through the *real* Catskills in mid-August was a virtual biker's wet dream, and two, he was well versed in the history of Woodstock. He knew most of the major roads coming off the New York State Thruway would, by now, be blocked with traffic jams up to ten miles long, making the long way around a shortcut. Will, his hair blowing in the wind, was blissfully unaware of these details.

***

In time, the road became a highway, and the highway a maze of abandoned cars, a jumbled pathway for the endless parade of freaks drifting toward the music. Chrome somehow threaded the needle through a cloud of Brown Buddha and patchouli and reached the outskirts of the magic city by sundown, where he gunned the weary Triumph up a grassy hillside and set her free beneath an ancient apple tree. A chocolate spliff emerged from behind Will's ear, and he offered Chrome a taste to get the party started. Chrome, who could get no higher, declined.

"Ready to take a dip in the cosmic sea?" Will, already glassy-eyed and jangled from the road, seemed to be caught off guard by the immensity of the crowd stretching out before them. His fingers danced nervously around the pendant resting on his breast.

"This is for you, Will; these are your people. I'm just along for the ride. When you come back down to earth, though, the sun and I will be here to greet you…stone solid." In the embrace that followed, the energy in Chrome's aura provided a bracing jolt of clarity to Will's drug-addled brain, but it was soon forgotten.

"See you in the morning dew, my brother," Will said, his smile shifting like the ground beneath his feet. With that, he turned and waded into the crowd as a new band lit up the sky with a tune so fine he felt like he was goin' up the country on a hot summer's day. He made his way through the sticky-sweet clouds of smoke and pheromones, moving sweat to sweat with countless bodies in the night. Then, somewhere in the zone between the Dead and the Family Stone, he fell into a trance and began to dance, his soul adrift in karmic bliss, free to fuck the angels of his dreams for all eternity. They were scattered all about him on the naked earth, half a million strong.

As the night wore on, his sense of wonder wore off. Without a vision or a dream or an angel to sustain him, he was hit head-on by the roaring darkness, which came crashing through his makeshift skull like a boulder from the moon, turning his tangle of utopian fantasies into a night on Bald Mountain. He found himself falling through the surface of the earth, trapped on a flaming freight elevator with an entire army of earthlings, and not a one of them could hear his screams. When he finally hit bottom, the only one left was Andy, way up in the sky, with diamonds.

The crowded dawn found Will, bleary-eyed, winding his way back to the only patch of clarity he could remember, where Chrome sat rapping under the apple tree with a small band of beaded nomads. Will, all scorched and sated, slithered into the circle, hunkering down to mine the vibes while trying to block out the sound of a dormouse screaming through the trees, telling him to *feed his head!*

* * *

"But how the fuck do you *know* that, man?" a bronzed, bearded gypsy in fringed and beaded buckskin was saying heatedly to the heavy-metal angel, his tribe of fellow gypsies scattered in a rough circle behind him.

"It was blowin' in the wind," Chrome said, and the gypsies burst into laughter.

"Yeah, well, Wavy Gravy just announced we're now the third-largest city in the state," the buckskinned fellow said.

"Look, I didn't say you couldn't change the world; I said it's unlikely you'll change it for the better. Every person on this planet is descended from hundreds of thousands of bad attitudes, and the undoing of that collective blindness is a task far beyond your newfound wisdom. Sorry." The circle erupted in protest.

"You can't be serious, man. We rode in here on a wave of peace, love, and harmony. We have instant karma on our side. Once that bolt of enlightenment hits, this'll be a whole new planet." Plenty of amens from the circle of gypsies.

"What you call enlightenment is not for the faint-hearted, and certainly not for amateurs. Rebellion is just as blind as obedience, so watch out; it can be quite a shock when the lights go on."

"Hey, man, where you *been*? Haven't you heard of acid? Here we are at the dawning of a new fucking age, and all you want to do is *paint it black!* I feel sorry for you, man. I really do." With that, the gypsy stood up and started down the hill, with his people a few steps behind. Chrome watched them wander off, as Will inched over and lay down on the grass beside him.

"What the hell was *that* all about?"

"Not much; just another debate about the shadows on the cave wall. How was your night in the garden of earthly delights?"

"Lotsa rain, but no lightning."

"Relax, Will. There are plenty of storms up ahead."

"No thanks, man; had one too many. Time to anchor off in some nice, quiet lagoon."

Chrome stood, stretched, reached into his pocket,

and pulled out a dazzlingly smooth, perfectly round white stone with the soft warm glow and translucent purity of ancient alabaster, no bigger than a wild cherry.

"Is *this* what you were looking for?" he said. His eyes twinkled as he held it up, then dropped it into the palm of Will's hand. Will stood transfixed as a strange warm glow, unlike anything he had felt before, began to spread through his body. Chrome smiled, turned, and headed downhill toward the bike.

"Let's roll, Willie Boy; we're headin' home."

13

PURGATORIO

In one last, desperate attempt to defy the laws of emotional gravity, Mona Lisa and her friends whisked Will into the heart of New Jersey for a weekend retreat at the Soul Integration Center, a sprawling estate once owned by a New York art dealer, now a fountain of instant karma for a new age of Aquarians. She thought the off-tempo mix of primal scream therapy and immersive tantric yoga would be just the thing to jar his demons loose, but from the moment he took his place in the circle of hungry souls, the unbridled howling felt even worse than the Rorschach treatment he had just received at the Echo Factory.

Many of his fellow supplicants were women from the Upper East Side, still brittle from the Fifties, hoping to join the sexual revolution before it all petered out. Others were mere window shoppers—spiritual tourists scouting out the latest in designer religions. But there was also a small cadre of authentic spiritual desperadoes—people whose lives hung in the balance—people like Will, who was trying frantically to reach the safety of nirvana without getting his ego bruised.

God's mercy finally arrived in the form of an earnest young man with the hair and jawline of a comic book superhero. Stepping into the center of the circle and bowing toward each of the cardinal directions in turn, hands joined above the heart chakra, he invited one and all to disrobe and join him in the sacred waters, which was basically a heated pool nestled inside a chamber of glass in an adjoining section of the compound.

As night fell in the outer world, they undressed in awkward silence and folded their earthly garments on their meditation cushions. Following the lead of their new superhero, they formed a loose line and began to giggle their way across a wooden foot-bridge leading toward a soft blue glow in the summer night. There, in the middle of a clearing, they came upon a steamy cathedral lit from within by the under-water lights of a shimmering lagoon surrounded by a jungle of flowering tropical plants. The air was dense with the musky scent of sandalwood incense as they slipped into the silky waters, uttering moans of joy.

Will lingered at the edge for a moment before sliding beneath the surface, emerging seconds later in the middle of the pool. He floated on his back through a fog of murmuring into a world of liquid wonder, where soft inner parts of the body proper, long constrained by the weight of civilization, were primed to unleash the secret longings that lurk within us all.

A fetching, blond madonna of childbearing age stood shoulder-deep in the center of it all, her beatific face beaming rays of cosmic love into the mist. As Will drifted by, she reached out and captured him in her arms, then reeled him in and held him tight, like a cherub on the belly of the midnight sky. He folded into her softness, his eager mouth searching for the source of sustenance. As she stiffened in his mouth, he grew hard in her hand.

She kissed him deeply and tenderly on the lips and then began moving slowly toward the epicenter, which by now was fully erect. Thus, by suckling the child, the woman gave birth to the man, who began the cycle anew, sending waves of love crashing against the sides of the pool. When the coupling was complete, they kissed and came undone. Will began to drift through the clusters of saints and sinners on his way to the deep end, where he stopped for a moment to observe the frenzy, then closed his eyes and sank beneath the surface to ponder the emptiness of his existence.

The magic of his slo-mo descent into silence seemed to bring him back to his right mind, the mind he had occasionally glimpsed while orbiting Chromium and Juliette. "This world is far from perfect," he thought, "but what if there really is another one? A better one, on a higher plane, with far less pain and struggle?" Ever since his encounters with them, he had begun to consider this a distinct possibility, and now, in the otherworldliness of his watery chamber, he began to realize that a chance for a new life had been offered him. All he had to do was stay alive long enough to find the signs, and follow the bread crumbs into the next chapter of his life.

At the last possible moment, he pushed hard against the blue concrete and rocketed back to the surface, gasping for air. After climbing out of the pool he grabbed a towel and padded back over the footbridge to the meditation room, alone, to wait for the session to end. During the long drive home, he tried to explain to Mona Lisa that, although he appreciated her concern for him (they had been apart for a while but remained friends), all it had done was remind him once again that it was impossible to fuck your way out of the darkness, and that scream-ing didn't help much either. After that, silence. He didn't mention his underwater revelation, thinking she might not understand. When she finally dropped him off at the studio, she kissed him on the cheek and said, wistfully, "I hope you find your angel, Will. I'd love to see you fly." He didn't know it then, but it would be the very last time he would see her.

＊

The next morning, he packed his belongings in an old army duffle bag, took one last look at the empty studio and set forth into the world, floating like an Indian sadhu through the darkening streets of the city, searching for a soul to hold on to, crashing wherever he could find an empty couch or a willing bedmate. The space between sanctuaries soon became longer, as friends grew weary of his muddled presence, or drifted away from the city themselves, desperate for fresh air and safety. But for Will, there was no way out, nowhere left to go. To stay afloat, he tripped some, smoked some, sold some, then tripped some more. Come night, he often fell asleep clutching the silver pendant, praying for the coming light.

On one of those nights, desperate for love and salvation, he dropped in at a party in the West Village, and there, hidden among the literati and the cognoscenti, he found a sweet little Nuyorican chica named Juanita, who spoke directly to his soul in the language of the streets. After a few hours alone together in a corner of the crowded room, she took him back to her joyous digs on 4th Street and kept him warm for the winter with her bed and her cuchifritos and her Ray Baretto records, the de facto soundtrack to their tumultuous lives. But this was a rescue project, and she knew it. She was the *mamacita*, a spicy dish of molten lava, ever ready to ignite the world, and he was the Black Irish poet with the broken wing. It had to end badly. As long as he was with her, there was no need to fly.

***

The letters from Dante began arriving in late winter, just as the melting snow began to expose the mountains of trash lining the streets of the city. They came in a flurry, sometimes two or three at a time, but once Will had scanned the acid-fueled hieroglyphics on both sides of that first envelope, he simply tossed the rest into his duffel bag. He figured Dante, like many of his fellow dharma bums, had gotten lost in the woods, and he was not about to launch a search party. Besides, they hadn't spoken in years. They had been roommates in college, but their friendship had come to a crashing halt in the middle of a star-tangled joyride across America, making his letters even more of an enigma.

In fact, the last time he'd laid eyes on him was in the orchards of the San Gabriel Valley, where the two of them had stopped to pick blood oranges for some quick cash before rolling into Los Angeles in Dante's midnight-blue Mustang fastback. They came undone one drunken night over a pretty little Mexican girl whose name Will couldn't even remember. Dante, brazenly invoking his Mediterranean roots, said there was no way he was going to share her with an Irish Mick, and so the next morning they were gone, headed west in the Mustang, leaving Will stranded in the orange groves. Judging by the postmark on the letters, it would appear he ended up in Palo Alto.

One day, confined to the apartment by a rare late-winter snow storm, Will decided to study the letters in depth. Perched on a windowsill overlooking the street, with both feet on the radiator and the letters in his lap, he began to open them one by one. Working chronologically, he pored over them, searching for clues to their meaning. With each successive page, he began to feel as though he were reading an illuminated manuscript, written in an unknown language—it *was* English after all, but it was arranged visually, as if the patterns meant as much as the words—a kind of pyroglyphics. Reading them was like eavesdropping on someone speaking to himself in tongues.

These were not letters in the ordinary sense, where word follows word, line follows line, all streaming forward to some final resting place where conclusions could be drawn and meanings could be gleaned. There was none of that. In fact, there was no order in any ordinary human sense. Words went flying in all directions, some glancing off one another in a zigzagging spiral while others went tramping up and down the page in a ragged column like a marching band full of margaritas. There were puns, double entendres, scraps of Dylan songs, obscure references to Hindu scripture, all buried in impenetrable word clusters—dense messages etching themselves directly onto the frosted window of his mind until, suddenly, it all became clear: it was the language of the angels, the voice of God.

"He's reached a state of beatific madness," Will thought. "He's a holy fool, channeling a blizzard of divine simultaneity into the mind of a hungry seeker." Once he had cracked the code of the mysterious letters, he read through them once more and put all the pieces of the puzzle together in his head. Dante had found a doorway to nirvana, and acid was the key. "Hey, this is America, right?" he thought. "Why torture yourself with yoga or meditation when you can just press a button and the door opens, drop a pill and the lights go on? Why not kickstart evolution with some instant karma?" Will was all in.

Though he didn't know it at the time, he was about to be cracked open like an egg and tossed onto a frying pan. But this was all he had, these were the bread crumbs that had been scattered in the forest, and so he convinced himself that this was the sign he was waiting for, a sign foreshadowed by the visitations of Chromium and Juliette. It no longer mattered that he hadn't seen either one of them for months and that they could not, apparently, be summoned; they must have been working behind the scenes all along, he figured, and had arranged for him to meet the One, the True and Living God, and, *Holy Hallelujah,* he was heading home at last!

***

All this happened while Will was staying and playing with Juanita down on 4th Street, and it only served to heat things up. She had let him in when the streets were cold and the sex was hot, but now it was going nowhere and, one way or another, a change was gonna come. His constant babbling about meeting God and going to the Promised Land had just about worn her out. "God ain't payin' the bills, Willy, so from now on, no money, no honey," she screamed in the heat of their final blowup.

"Love ain't nothin' but a firecracker, mamacita; blink once and it's gone," he mumbled as he packed his things, shuffled out the door and headed down the piss-stained stairwell, shivering cold into the dirty wet snow of a dying winter.

"Life is full of purgatories," he thought, "gulags of the soul, way stations where you say your prayers and do your time for the sins of your father and, if you're lucky, move on to the next big slice of darkness. But, man, I'm finally breaking out of this goddam prison. If only Daddy could see me now" He was smiling for the first time in a long while as he slid into the back seat of the battered yellow cab, touching the silver pendant gently as the taxi began whipsawing through the snow, suddenly shooting forward when it hit raw pavement. The cabbie called to him over the front seat.

"Where ya headed, buddy?"

"Paradise, man; take me to paradise." Will was still smiling at the thought of his big adventure.

Juliette, after witnessing these events from afar, zoomed in and hovered above the empty street, watching as the taxi took its place in the endlessly churning traffic down on Avenue A. She wished with every pixel of her being that she could drop from the sky like Wonder Woman and stop the cab with her bare hands, but she knew that this was how it had to be. She knew deep in her heart that the only way for Will to reach Channel Two was to pass through the inferno, to be stripped right down to the mainframe and rebuilt from the ground up. A single crystal tear rolled down her cheek. This was her first taste of human love, and it hurt like hell.

A PERFECT BLUE FIRE

Somewhere along the vast circle of time, Chrome lay dreaming on the cool halocrete surface of the sky platform. It was the eve of his final show in SubVersa—a retrospective of the works that had brought him fame and glory, a trove of visual thought experiments that had carried him to the peak of his creative powers. It was an otherworldly art made of math and pixel dust, limited only by the range of his imagination and his fluency in the living language of code. Chrome, it was said, could write in tongues.

But rather than reveling in past glories, he found himself daydreaming about the mission ahead, the mysterious work of soulmining, and the dangers he might face in the atomic world. On the surface, it might appear that his art career had come to an end, but he now understood that his greatest work of art was *himself*, and there was much more work to be done. Come morning, he would sync his energies with Juliette's, shift their creative powers into overdrive, and begin focusing on the well-spring of their own being—their souldriver, Will Powers. His thoughts were suddenly punctuated by the flash of a brilliant blue comet streaking across the midnight sky.

Seconds later, she appeared above him, hovering; an angel in black satinelle; midnight wings aflutter, violet eyes beaming, dusky-rose lips on moonlit skin. Treading air like a ballerina, she casually descended on him in a slo-mo blur, all feathers and fingers of light. There was motion, heat, then stillness. Twice warmed, they lay together soundlessly, drenched in starlight, soaking up the black-velvet night. Chrome broke the spell by whispering into her hair.

"That comet…That was you, wasn't it?"

"Mmm, lovely thought. I'll tuck that one under my pillow," she said dreamily.

Though her true powers were hidden beneath that glow-in-the-dark smile, he was fully aware of her capabilities. She had been conceived in the Celestial City in a rare collaboration between Quin and his own maker, Will (who by then was an old man, in human terms, and already prepping for convergence), and because they had chosen to deliver her into this world through the streaming power of his own mind, he was intimately acquainted with every feature of her system and had, from the start, held her in awe.

When Quin was preparing to write the code for her personality, for instance, she calibrated the most exquisite feminine aspects of Will's being, carefully interweaving them with the fiery algorithms of a Code Warrior princess. The entire construct was then primed to interface with Chrome's masculine creative template. When the full-blown engine of her AI was complete and the entire database of neural history was uploaded, she became a glimmering, shimmering, creative machine, designed to gobble up new data from the minute she was turned on, scanning endlessly in search of new patterns and possibilities.

"Going up against the creators of Dark Math will be a challenge," he said, "but with you by my side, it won't be an insurmountable one."

"When we're running in tandem, Chrome, we're unbeatable. You're my Chrometheus, the one to my zero; together we're a font of digital procreation. We'll make the Nomads look like a bunch of high school griefers."

"Yes, yes, and yes; glad to have you riding shot-gun, honey."

"You know, Chrome, sometimes I find myself wishing I'd been here all along, working with you from the beginning, whispering in your ear when you made all this magic. I often wonder what we might have created together…," she said wistfully.

"I often wonder that myself. But the timing of your arrival wasn't up to me; I needed a bit more polishing, it seems. I wasn't quite ready for you in the beginning."

"Did you miss me before you met me?"

"Miss you? I missed you so much I tried to make you."

"But how? When?"

Taking a deep breath, he recounted the story of Neon in flaming detail, from the days and nights he spent building her in the studio, all the way down to his final moments with Raven. It was a long, hard fall, as he recalled, and he barely survived the impact. But it was worth it, he said, for the *real thing* was now lying right here in his arms, and he never would have known just how real she was if he hadn't been forced to walk that last mile over the burning coals of human love. And her skin was so cool to the touch.

After a long silence, Juliette spoke, softly. "I've never experienced that kind of heartache, Chrome, and I'm sorry you had to go through it. But now all of that is behind us and we're ready to fully engage with the future."

"So we're still fine, Q?" he asked, like a man out on a limb who hears the sound of a chainsaw.

"Fine for all time, babe," she said, nuzzling the soft undercoat of his gleaming metal hair.

"Then we're headed for the future; are you down for the struggle?" His question drew her to an upright position.

"Ready as you are, Comandante, and not a moment too soon. Now that Will's dreams of art stardom have gone up in smoke, he's being drawn to a much hotter flame than a simple quest for fame: a long lost friend is luring him to the West Coast with a promise of instant enlightenment. According to the data, this is where he begins drifting away from the herd to graze on the fringes of human identity, test the limits of human understanding. Unfortunately, it's a terrifying thing for a human being to step outside the zeitgeist, and the further he wanders, the higher the risk of suicide or madness.

Unfortunately, it's the only way to scrub the code before the upgrade."

"We'll be there, Q. But timing will be everything; we have to get in before the digital dogs of Cyberia descend on him and drive him back to the herd."

"Exactly. Keep him safe until the upgrade is complete, while giving him enough strength to endure the process. But just think about it, Chrome—when all this is over, the three of us will be one, launched like an Apollo rocket, co-starring in an endless theater of the mind and streaming the new infinity, live on Channel Three."

"Amen to that, honey. Hallowed be thy game."

Thus, the artist and his muse lay suspended between two great epochs of their lives. They spent the rest of that night reminiscing about their days and nights in paradise and dreaming of the road ahead, eventually slipping into deep sleep mode enfolded in one another's arms. Their new lives would dawn soon enough.